William H. G. Kingston

The Settlers

A Tale of Virginia

William H. G. Kingston

The Settlers
A Tale of Virginia

ISBN/EAN: 9783337241100

Printed in Europe, USA, Canada, Australia, Japan

Cover: Foto ©Andreas Hilbeck / pixelio.de

More available books at **www.hansebooks.com**

THE SETTLERS:

A TALE OF VIRGINIA.

BY

WILLIAM H. G. KINGSTON.

PUBLISHED UNDER THE DIRECTION OF THE
COMMITTEE OF GENERAL LITERATURE AND EDUCATION, APPOINTED BY
THE SOCIETY FOR PROMOTING CHRISTIAN KNOWLEDGE.

LONDON:
Society for Promoting Christian Knowledge.
Sold at the Depositories:
77, Great Queen Street, Lincoln's Inn Fields;
4, Royal Exchange; 48, Piccadilly;
And by all Booksellers.
NEW YORK: POTT, YOUNG, & CO.

The Settlers

IN COLOURS BY W. DICKES

CICELY LAYTON.

Page 20.

TURTLES COMING ON SHORE.

Page 71.

POWHATTAN AND HIS DAUGHTER.

Page 132.

MANITA IN THE CANOE.

Page 169.

THE SETTLERS:

A Tale of Virginia.

CHAPTER I.

THE abode of Captain Amyas Layton over-looked the whole of Plymouth Sound. It stood on the eastern side near its north-ern end, on the wood-covered heights which rise above that magnificent estuary. From

the windows could be seen the town of Plymouth, with its inner harbour, on which floated many a stout bark of varied rig and size ; some engaged in the coasting trade, others just arrived from foreign voyages, and others destined to carry the flag of England to far-off lands. In front of the house had been set up a tall flagstaff, which the captain was wont on high days and holidays to deck with gay banners, or at other times to employ in making signals to vessels in the Sound. The grounds were surrounded by a moat with a drawbridge, above which was a gateway adorned with curiously carved images once serving as the figure-heads of two Spanish galleys. The house itself, constructed chiefly of a framework of massive timber, filled in with stone or brick, had no pretensions to architectural beauty, albeit its wide, projecting eaves, its large chimneys, and latticed windows, with its neat, well-kept garden full of gay flowers, gave it a picturesque and quaint appearance. Above the low wall on the inner side of the moat, was planted a battery of brass cannon, elaborately ornamented, and evidently also taken from the Spaniards; though they were placed there as trophies of victories won rather than for use. In truth, the old seaman's dwelling, full as it was of many other warlike engines, had no pretensions to the character of a fortress; it had been his fancy to gather within its walls the spoils of many a hard-fought fight to remind him of days gone by, especially when he had sailed out of Plymouth Sound in his stout bark in company with the gallant Lord Howard, Drake, Frobisher, Hawkins, and other brave seamen whose names are known to fame, to make fierce onslaught on the vaunting Spaniards, as their proud Armada swept up the Channel. The porch at the front entrance was adorned with Spanish handiwork—a portion of the stern-gallery of the huge *St. Nicholas;* while at each corner of the building were fixed other parts of that mighty galleon, or of some other ship of the many which had been, by God's good providence, delivered into the hands of those whom the haughty Spaniards came vainly threatening to enslave.

The house contained a good-sized dining-hall. At one end was a broad fireplace, and mantelpiece supported by richly carved figures, also taken from the stern-gallery of a Spanish bark. Above it appeared the model of the *Golden Lion*, the captain's own ship. The walls were adorned with breastplates and morions, swords and matchlocks, huge pistols, with other weapons of curious form, and three banners captured from the foe, regarded by the captain as the chiefest of his trophies. Here, too, were also bows and arrows, spears and clubs, and various implements, remembrances of the last voyage he had made to America.

The captain was walking to and fro in the shade. In his hand was a long pipe with a huge bowl, from which he ever and anon sucked up a mouthful of smoke, which, as he again puffed it out, rose in light wreaths above his head. Sometimes, as he sent them forth slowly, now from one side of his mouth, now from the other, as a ship fires her broadsides at her foes, he would stop and gaze at the vanishing vapour, his thoughts apparently wandering to distant times and regions far away, now taking a glance down the Sound to watch for any tall ship which might be coming up from the westward, now looking along the road.

His countenance, though that of a man still hale and hearty, showed signs of many a hard fight with human foes and fierce storms, as far as it could be distinguished amid the curling locks which hung down from beneath the low-crowned hat adorned by a single feather, and the bushy beard and long mustachios still but slightly grizzled. His doublet and cloak were richly embroidered, though the gold lace was somewhat tarnished; his breeches, fastened

at the knee, were of ample proportions, while boots of buskin form encased his feet. A man of war from his youth, though enjoying his ease, he even now wore girded to his side his trusty sword without which he was never known to stir outside his door.

At length he stopped; as his eye glanced along the road leading from Plymouth. "Marry, who can those be coming up the hill?" he said to himself. "They seem to be making for this—a well-grown youth and a youngster—by their habits and appearance they are I judge of gentle birth." As he spoke, the captain advanced towards the gateway to give the young strangers a welcome, should it be their purpose to pay him a visit. The elder was of a tall and graceful figure, with delicate features, a slight moustache appearing on his lip; his habit, that of a gallant of the day, though modest and free from extravagance.

The younger was of a stronger build; his countenance exhibiting a bold and daring spirit, full of life and animation, and not wanting in good-humour.

" Whom seek you, young sirs ? " asked the old seaman, as the youths drew near.

" One Captain Amyas Layton, an please you, sir," answered the elder of the two. " We were told in Plymouth town, where we arrived last night on horseback from Dartmouth, that we should find his residence in this direction ; and if I mistake not, we stand even now before him."

" You are right in your conjectures, young sirs," answered Captain Layton ;" I am the man you seek, and whoever you are and whatever your object, believing it to be an honest one, I give you greeting. Enter, for after your walk this warm summer's day you need rest and refreshment ; the first you may take at once—the second you shall have as soon as my daughter Cicely returns from Plymouth, whither she has gone a-marketing, with our servant Barnaby, on our old nag Sampson, which I called after a

Spanish carvel I sank out yonder—but of that anon. Come in."

The captain, without waiting to make further inquiries of the strangers, led the way into the hall, where he bade them take their seats in two carved oak chairs on either side of the fireplace—albeit the warmth of the day permitted not a fire to be burning there. The young men, removing their beavers, obeyed him.

"Though more substantial fare be wanting, I can serve you with a stoup of Canary, young sirs; and your walk, judging by my own taste, will render such acceptable," said the captain. Assuring him that they were in no way fatigued, they declined the wine on the plea of the early hour, and their not having been in the habit of drinking aught except a glass of ale at dinner or supper.

"A prudent custom for those not advanced in life," he observed; "and now, young sirs, to what cause am I indebted for this visit?"

"We have a long story to narrate, kind sir," answered the elder youth, "and we would first tell you our names, and whence we come; which, in your hospitable kindness, you have not yet inquired. We are the sons of your old shipmate Captain Vaughan Audley, who, it has been supposed for the last ten years or more, perished among those who formed the first settlement in Virginia, planted by the brave Sir Walter Raleigh. For that long period our dear mother, notwithstanding the reports which reached her, has never altogether abandoned the hope that he might be alive ; and though compelled to assume widow's weeds, she has remained faithful to his memory and refused again to wed."

" A true wife and honest woman, such as I delight to honour," observed the captain; " but alack ! I received too certain news of my old comrade's death to make me doubt that he had passed away to that better land where we all hope to meet."

" Truly, our mother, notwithstanding her expressions to the contrary, had begun to believe the same," answered the young man ; " when about ten days gone by, there came to the gate of our house near Dartmouth, where we have lived since our father's departure, a seaman somewhat advanced in life, whose pallid face spoke of sickness, and his tattered garments of poverty long suffered. His name, he told us, was Richard Batten. He had wandered, he said, over all parts of the known globe; but though his pockets had been often filled with Spanish gold, they had again been quickly emptied through his own folly, and the greed of pretended friends ; gambling, drinking, and other similar pursuits being his bane. He now begged a crust and a draught of beer, or even of water, with leave to lie down in an outhouse that he might rest his weary limbs. We listened to his sad tale, and being sure that he spoke the truth, invited him into the house and placed before him a hearty meal, to which, however, he seemed scarcely able to do justice, so far gone was he with sickness. Still the little he ate revived him, and he talked on with my brother Gilbert here—a ready listener. At

first he spoke only of voyages made long ago, but at
length he told him of one he had lately performed
across the Atlantic in a ship to obtain sassafras, and
trade with the natives of Virginia. The name immediately aroused Gilbert's attention, who called me to
listen to what the seaman was saying. He had sailed
in April from Milford Haven, on board the *Speedwell*,
Captain Martin Pring, a ship of about fifty tons,
the year after our present King James came to the
throne, and in company with her went the *Discoverer*, a
bark of the same size, commanded by Captain Brown.
They were victualled for eight months, and laden
with all sorts of apparel, gewgaws and baubles proper
to trade with the inhabitants of the country whither
they were going. Arriving off the coast of Virginia
in June, they entered a great gulf, where they found
people on both sides, with whom they had much
intercourse. Here they were engaged in loading
their bark with sassafras, much to their satisfaction.

" Batten, however, while searching for sassafras,
having wandered away from his companions, thinking to return, got yet farther from them, and
at length, overcome with fatigue, fell asleep. On
awaking he found that it was night. When daylight returned, clouds covered the sky, and, still
thinking to get back to the ship, he went on all
day, but again failed to see the great river in
which she rode.

" Having his gun and ammunition, he was able to
shoot some birds and animals, and with the fruits

he found growing on the trees he sustained life. Thus for three days more he wandered up and down, till he at length reached the river; when to his dismay, he could nowhere see the ship. Having no doubt that she had sailed, he now set off along the shore, hoping to overtake her in case she had brought up at any other place. He was pushing on bravely, when he saw before him a large party of Indians ; to fight with them was useless—he held out his hand, which the chief took, and showed by signs that he would be his friend. He tried to inquire for the ship, but the Indians made him understand that she had gone away and that it was best for him to remain with them. He thought so likewise, and agreed to live with them, and to hunt and fish as they did.

"After some time they set off up the country, where larger game was to be found. Having husbanded his powder, as long as that lasted he was able to shoot several deer ; but when that was gone, and he could no longer help the Indians, they treated him with less kindness than at first. This made him resolve to try and escape ; he had got some distance from their camp, when he encountered another party of Indians, of a different tribe to those with whom he had been living. They carried him off a long way through the woods, till they reached their camp, when he was taken before their chief. A council was held, as he supposed, to decide whether he was to live or to be put to death. He was fully expecting to die, when a person whom he had not before seen appeared, and addressed him. On looking up at the stranger's face, greatly to his surprise he saw that he was a white man. Batten inquired whom he was.

" 'A heart-broken exile—one who can feel for you,' was the answer ; ' but fear not for your life—for that I will plead, as I have interest with the chief, though for years I have been kept a prisoner without hope of escape.'

" Who think you, Captain Layton, was the stranger who now spoke to Batten ? He was no other than our father, Captain Vaughan Audley, who sailed with Sir Richard Grenville, Mr. Dane, and Mr. Cavendish on board the *Roebuck* with many other ships in company. When Sir Richard returned to England, our father had remained with upwards of a hundred men with Governor Dane at Roanoke, where they fixed their abode and built a fort. The Indians, who had hitherto been friendly, formed, however, a league against them. They were expecting assistance from England, when one night the fort was stormed; most of the people were put to the sword, but the life of our father was preserved by a chief whom he had befriended when, on a former occasion, that chief had fallen into the hands of the English. The chief, carrying him to his canoe, concealed him from his companions and conveyed him far away up the river. Here landing, he concealed him in his own wigwam, where he was cured of his hurts ; but our father had not from that time seen a white face till he met with Batten.

" Batten's life, as our father promised, was saved ; though the Indians showed otherwise but little regard for him, and this made him wish to escape should he have the opportunity. He told his purpose to our father, and promised, should he succeed, to carry home the intelligence to his friends of his being alive. Some time afterwards, Batten said, he managed to escape from the Indians, when he made his way towards the seashore. Lying hid in a thick bush for fear of being discovered by the natives, he one day caught sight of a party of Englishmen advancing at no great distance off. Delighted at the thoughts of meeting his countrymen, he was about to rush out of his place of concealment, when he saw a large body of Indians coming towards them. He waited to see the result, when to his horror the Indians drew their bows, and before the strangers were aware of their danger, every man among them was pierced by an arrow. Some fell dead ; others drew their swords; but with terrific war-whoops the Indians, setting on them, killed the whole with their tomahawks.

" Batten gave up all hopes of saving his life, but, wishing to put off the fatal moment, he remained concealed till near nightfall, when the Indians cutting off the scalps of the slain, went away inland, singing a song of triumph. He now stole out of his hiding-place, and ran on all night, intending to build a raft and make his way along the coast, when just at daybreak, as he reached the shore, great was his joy to discover an English boat with two men in her. He rushed towards them, and gave an account of the way he had seen the Englishmen murdered. No sooner did they hear this than they shoved off from the shore and pulled with all their might down the river. For several days they continued toiling, till they reached their bark, the *Sally Rose* which lay some way down towards its mouth; but the master, on hearing that the pilot and all the officers had been killed, forthwith weighed anchor, and, setting sail, stood for England. The *Sally Rose* sprang a leak, and scarcely could she be kept afloat till, coming up Channel, they entered the port of Dartmouth. Here landing, Batten was making his way without a groat in his pocket to London, when Providence directed him to our door.

" On hearing this strange narrative, I sent Gilbert to fetch our mother and sister Lettice, who listened to it with breathless interest; and getting such answers as we could from the seaman to the questions put to him, we were all convinced that he had given us a faithful account, and that our father was really alive. We now earnestly consulted with him what to do ; not forgetting to seek for guidance from on high as to the best means for recovering our father. Gilbert was for setting out forthwith, taking Batten as his companion, and getting on board the first ship sailing for America; but even had our mother agreed to Gilbert's proposal, it was impracticable, as the old sailor was becoming worse and worse. We sent for the apothecary, and did all we could to restore his waning strength; but all was in vain, and before the next day was over he had breathed his last.

"We were now much troubled, for the means on which we had depended for discovering our father had thus been lost. We had no one with whom to consult; we talked and talked, but could come to no conclusion. 'We will pray to God for guidance,' said our mother, 'we will now, my children, go to rest; and to-morrow morning we will meet, with the hope that light will be afforded us to direct our course.'

"Her first words the following morning when she entered the parlour were : 'Praise be to God—he has not left me any longer in doubt what to do—I have bethought me of Captain Amyas Layton, who resides not far from Plymouth. He and your father have often been shipmates, and he is among the oldest of his friends, and will give you sound advice on the subject. I would wish you to set out forthwith for Plymouth, and to place the whole matter before him. Tell him that I will expend all my means towards fitting out a ship to send to Virginia with trustworthy persons to search for your father. It may be, though, for the love Captain Layton bore him, that he will afford further means if necessary for the purpose.'"

"That will I right gladly," exclaimed the captain, starting up, and taking three or four paces between the chairs in which the young brothers were sitting—first looking at one and then at the other; "you two are Audleys—I recognize your father's features in both your countenances. There are few men whose

c

memory I hold in greater love or esteem, and I will
not say that to recover him I would hazard half my
fortune, for the whole of it I would gladly give to
bring him back, and old as I am, will sail forth
myself in command of a ship to Virginia should a
younger man of sufficient experience be wanting.
You, young sir, I perceive by your dress and looks,
have not been to sea ; or you would be the proper
person to sail in search of the missing one."

" No, sir," answered Vaughan, " but I have been
for some time a student at Cambridge, where I have
diligently studied mathematics, and being well
acquainted with the mode by which ships are navi-
gated, although I am ignorant of the duties of a seaman, I might, with the aid of a sailing master, be
able without difficulty to reach the country of which
Batten told us. Gilbert has already made two voyages
to the Thames, and one as far as the Firth of Forth,
so that he is not altogether ignorant of sea affairs,
and lacks not willingness for the purpose."

" So I should judge," observed the captain, casting
an approving look at Gilbert ; " I like your spirit,
young man ; and you may trust to me that I will do
all I can to forward your views. Had my son Roger
been at home, the matter might quickly have been
arranged ; but he has long been gone on a voyage
to the East Indies with Sir Edward Michaelbourn,
on board the *Tiger*, a stout ship, in which Captain
John Davis sailed as pilot. There went also a
pinnace named the *Tiger's Whelp*. I would the
good ship were back again, for Roger is my only

son, and his sister Cicely begins to fret about him."

" Gladly would I serve under your son, should he before long return and be willing to sail for Virginia," replied Vaughan.

" Would you be as willing to serve under me, young sir?" asked the captain, glancing from under his shaggy eyebrows at Vaughan; " for verily, should not Roger soon come back, I should be greatly inclined to fit out a stout ship, and take Cicely on board and all my household goods, and to settle down in the New World. Cicely has her brother's spirit, and will be well pleased to engage in such a venture; as I will promise her to leave directions for Roger to join us should he return after we have sailed."

" I could desire nothing better, Captain Layton," answered the young man; " our mother will indeed rejoice to hear that you have been so ready to comply with her request. What you propose far surpasses her expectations."

Captain Amyas Layton had been a man of action all his life, and age had not quenched his ardour. While pacing up and down, his thoughts were rapidly at work; every now and then he addressed his young guests, evidently turning over in his mind the various plans which suggested themselves.

" My old shipmate Captain George Weymouth is now in England," he said, " I will write to learn his opinion. I have another friend, Captain Bartholomew Gosnell. I know not if he has again sailed since his last voyage to America; if not, I will find him

c 2

out. He will, to a certainty, have useful information to give us."

Thus the captain ran over the names of various brave commanders, who had at different times visited the shores of North America. He counted much also, he said, on Captain John Davis, who had sailed along those coasts; though he had gained his chief renown in the northern seas, amid the ice-mountains which float there throughout the year—his name having been given to those straits through which he passed into that region of cold. Vaughan and Gilbert had been listening attentively to all he said, desiring to report the same to their mother and Lettice, when the sound of a horse's hoofs were heard in the paved yard by the side of the house.

" Here comes Cicely with Barnaby, and we shall ere long have dinner, for which I doubt not, my young friends, you will be ready," observed the captain.

Gilbert acknowledged that his appetite was becoming somewhat keen; but Vaughan made no remark. He was of an age to watch with some interest for the appearance of Mistress Cicely Layton, though of her existence he had not heard till her father mentioned her.

He had not long to wait before a side-door opened, and a young damsel with straw hat on head and riding-habit fitting closely to a graceful form, entered the hall. She turned a surprised glance at the strangers, and then gave an inquiring one at her father, who forthwith made known their guests to

her as the sons of an old friend ; on which she put
forth her hand and frankly welcomed them. The
colour of her cheek heightened slightly as Vaughan,
with the accustomed gallantry of the day, pressed her
hand to his lips, and especially as his eyes met hers
with a glance of admiration in them which her beauty
had inspired. Truly, Cicely Layton was a maiden
formed in nature's most perfect mould—at least, so
thought Vaughan Audley. Gilbert also considered
her a very sweet girl, though not equal in all
respects to his sister Lettice, who was fairer
and somewhat taller and more graceful; but then
Gilbert always declared that Lettice was perfection
itself.

Having delivered certain messages she had
brought from Plymouth for her father, Cicely addressed a few remarks to the young gentlemen ;
then, saying that she must go to prepare for serving
up the dinner, which, as it was near noon, ought
soon to be on the table, she dropped a courtesy and
left the room. Each time the door opened, Vaughan
turned his eyes in that direction, expecting to see
Mistress Cicely enter; but first came a waiting-
maid to spread a damask table-cloth of snowy whiteness, and then came Barnaby Toplight with knives
and forks ; then Becky came back with plates.
"This must be she," thought Vaughan ; but no—it
was Barnaby again with a huge covered dish, followed
by Becky with other viands.

At length the door again opened, and Mistress
Cicely tripped in, her riding-dress laid aside. She

was habited in silken attire, her rich tresses falling back from her fair brow, her neck surrounded by a lace ruff of wondrous whiteness. The captain having said grace, desired his guests to fall to on the viands placed before them; though Vaughan seemed often to forget to eat, while conversing with Mistress Cicely; Gilbert meantime finding ample subject for conversation with her father.

Dinner occupied no great length of time, though the captain insisted on his friends sitting with him to share a bottle of Canary, which he ordered Barnaby to bring from the cellar, that they might drink success to their proposed voyage to Virginia. The young men then rose, offering to return to Plymouth, but their host would on no account hear of it, declaring that they must remain till he could see certain friends in Plymouth with whom he desired to consult about their projected voyage. They without hesitation accepted his proffered hospitality; possibly the satisfaction the elder felt in Mistress Cicely's company might have assisted in deciding him to remain, instead of returning home. Indeed, he considered it would be better to wait, that he might carry some certain information to his mother as to the progress made in the matter.

In the evening Mistress Cicely invited him to stroll forth into the neighbouring woods, beneath whose shade the sea-breeze which rippled the surface of the Sound might be fully enjoyed. Their conversation need not be repeated; for Cicely talked much of her gallant brother, and was sure that

Master Audley would be well pleased to make his acquaintance when he should return from the East Indies. "Though, alack! I know not when that will be," she added, with a sigh.

The captain and Gilbert followed, talking on various interesting subjects. The captain was highly pleased with Gilbert, who reminded him greatly of his father.

"I knew him when he was no older than you are," observed the former. "A right gallant youth he was. Already he had been in two or more battles, and had made two voyages to the Spanish main. He married young, and I thought would have given up the ocean; but, like many others, was tempted to go forth in search of fortune, intending, I believe, that your mother should follow when he had founded a home for her in the Western World."

"I have heard my mother say, sir," said Gilbert, "that my father was but twenty-five when he sailed for Virginia, leaving me an infant, and my brother and sister still small children; so that even my brother has no recollection of his appearance."

The captain had led Gilbert to a knoll, a favourite resort, whence he could gaze over the Sound far away across its southern entrance. He pulled out his pipe and tobacco-pouch from his capacious pocket, and began, as was his wont, to smoke right lustily, giving utterance with deliberation, at intervals, as becomes a man thus employed, to various remarks touching the matter in hand. He soon found that Gilbert, young as he was, possessed a fair amount of nautical knowledge, and was not ignorant of the higher branch of navigation, which he had studied while at home, with the assistance of his brother Vaughan.

"You will make a brave seaman, my lad, if Heaven wills that your life is preserved," observed Captain Layton; "all you want is experience, and on the ocean alone can you obtain that."

"Had it not been for the unwillingness of my mother to part with me, I should have gone ere this on a long voyage," answered Gilbert. "It was not without difficulty that she would consent to my making the short trips of which I have told you; though now that I have a sacred duty to perform, she will allow me to go. As we were unable to obtain the exact position of the region where Batten met our father, we must expect to encounter no small amount of difficulty and labour before we discover him."

"We must search for the crew of the vessel in which Batten returned, for they may be able to give us the information we require," observed the captain; and he further explained how he proposed setting about making the search.

While he had been speaking, Gilbert's eye had been turned towards the south-west. "Look there, sir!" he exclaimed, suddenly; "I have been for some time watching a ship running in for the Sound, and I lately caught sight of a smaller one following her."

"I see them, my lad; they are standing boldly on, as if they well knew the port," said the captain. "I fear lest my hopes may mock me, but this is about the time I have been expecting my son, who sailed with John Davis for India, to return, unless any unexpected accident should have delayed them. Those two ships are, as far as I can judge at this distance, the size of the *Tiger* and the *Tiger's Whelp*."

Still the captain sat on, yet doubting whether he was right. The ships rapidly approached, for the wind was fresh and fair. Now they came gliding up the Sound, the larger leading some way ahead of the smaller. The captain, as he watched them, gave expression to his hopes and doubts.

"See! see! sir," exclaimed Gilbert, whose eyes were unusually sharp; "there is a flag at the main-mast-head of the tall ship. On it I discern the figure of a tiger, and if I mistake not, the smaller bears one of the same description."

"Then there can be no doubt about the matter," exclaimed Captain Layton. "We will at once return home. Go find your brother and my daughter; tell them the news, and bid them forthwith join us."

While the captain walked on to the house, Gilbert went, as he was directed, in search of Vaughan and Cicely. They, too, had been seated on a bank some way further on, watching the ships, but neither had suspected what they were. Indeed, so absorbed were they in their own conversation, that they had not even observed Gilbert's approach. Cicely started when she heard his voice, and on receiving the intelligence he brought, rose quickly, and, accompanied by the brothers, hastened homewards.

"The news seems almost too good to be true; but, alack!" she added, with a sigh, as if the thought had just struck her, "suppose he is not on board—what a blow will it be to my poor father! Roger is his only son; and he has ever looked forward with pride to the thought of his becoming a great navigator like Sir Francis Drake or Sir Thomas Cavendish."

Vaughan endeavoured to reassure her.

"My fears are foolish and wrong," said Cicely; "but if you knew how we love him, and how worthy he is of our love, you would understand my anxious fears as to his safety."

"I can understand them, and sympathize with you fully," said Vaughan. His reply seemed to please her.

On reaching the house, they found that the captain had already gone down to the beach, where his boat lay; and, his anxiety not allowing him to wait for the young men, he had rowed off to the headmost ship, which had now come to an anchor, the crew being busily engaged in furling sails. Poor Cicely had thus a still longer time to wait till her anxiety was relieved, or till she might learn the worst. She insisted on going down to the beach, to which Vaughan and Gilbert accompanied her. At length the captain's skiff was seen to leave the side of the ship. He had gone by himself, but now they discovered, when the skiff got nearer the shore, another person, who stood up and waved a handkerchief. Cicely clasped her hands, then cried out with joy, "It is Roger! it is Roger!" and presently, the boat reaching the shore, Roger leaped out, and his sister was clasped in his arms.

Releasing herself, she introduced him to Vaughan and Gilbert, of whom he had already heard from his father, as well as the object of their visit. "And so, young sirs, you have work cut out for me, I understand, and intend not to let the grass grow under my feet," he exclaimed, in a hearty tone. "All I can say is that I am ready to follow my father's wishes in the matter."

" I am truly thankful to you, sir," replied
Vaughan, as he and Roger shook hands; and
looking in each other's faces, they both thought,
" we shall be friends." Vaughan admired Roger's
bold and manly countenance, possessing, as it
did, a frank and amiable expression; his well-
knit frame showing him to be the possessor
of great strength; while Roger thought Vaughan
a noble young fellow, of gentle breeding.

The young men having assisted in securing the
skiff, the party returned to the house, where Roger
gave them a brief account of his voyage, for the
captain was eager to know how it had fared with
him.

They had, however, matter of more pressing importance to talk about, and before they retired to
rest that night, their plans for the future had been
discussed, and some which were afterwards carried
out had been determined on.

CHAPTER II.

AUGHAN and Gilbert consented to remain with their friends another day, on condition that Roger Layton would accompany them to their home, in order to explain more fully than they could do the plans he and his father proposed. In truth, Vaughan was not sorry for the opportunity afforded him of enjoying more of Cicely's society, and he knew Mistress Audley did not expect their speedy return. Roger undertook afterwards to proceed to London to search for the *Sally Rose*, a bark of fifty tons, in which Batten had returned home, and which Vaughan had learnt had gone round to the Thames.

The more Captain Layton talked over the matter, the more his ancient ardour revived. " Cicely, girl, wilt thou go with me?" he exclaimed. " I cannot leave thee behind; and yet I should fret if these young gallants were away searching for my brave friend and I were to remain on shore, like a weather-beaten old hulk, unfit for further service."

" Where you go, I will go, my father, as you wish it," answered Cicely; " whether in Old England, or in New England across the ocean, there, if you make your home, will I gladly abide with you."

"Well said, girl, well said," exclaimed the captain; "come, let me give thee a buss for thy dutiful love—but I will not force thy inclinations."

The next day the captain, mounted on his horse Sampson, set off for Plymouth, the distance being too great for him to walk, in order to call on some of his seafaring acquaintances, and to make inquiries regarding vessels in the port of Plymouth and elsewhere, fit for a voyage to America. Roger and Gilbert accompanied him on foot, but Master Vaughan pleaded that, as he knew naught of naval affairs, he could be of no service, and would prefer remaining to study the captain's sea journals and some books on navigation, with the prospect of afterwards taking a stroll with Mistress Cicely when she should have completed her household duties for the day.

"As you like it," said the captain; "Cicely will bring you the books, and pens and paper, should you wish to take notes of what you read."

Cicely thought Vaughan's plan a very proper one, and it is possible that she hastened through her household duties with even more than her usual alacrity, active as she always was.

The captain, with his son and Gilbert, called on several persons, including among them some shipbuilders and shipowners, from one of whom they learnt that the *Rainbow*, a stout bark of a hundred tons burthen, lay in the harbour, having a short time before returned from the only voyage she had made to the Levant, her timbers and plankings sound, her tacklings and sails in perfect order ; moreover that, in two weeks or so, she might be got ready for sea. On going on board, the captain and his son were well pleased with the *Rainbow's* appearance, though of opinion that her tackling and sails required renewing, and that the necessary repairs would take longer than her owner had stated. The captain, as has been said, was a man of action ; having satisfied himself as to the fitness of the vessel, on returning on shore he concluded the purchase, with such deductions as were considered just by her owner, Master Holdfast, who, knowing him to be a man of substance as well as a man of honour, was content to abide his time with regard to payment.

The next day found Vaughan and Gilbert, accompanied by Roger Layton, on their way to the neighbourhood of Dartmouth. Lettice, who had been anxiously waiting for their return, seeing them come over the hill in the distance, hastened down to the gate to receive them. After bestowing on her an affectionate embrace, they introduced Roger as the son of their friend Captain Layton, returned from the Indies, who was ready to sail forth again in search of their father. It is needless to say that he received a warm welcome from Mistress Audley, as well as from Lettice. Roger had thought his sister Cicely was as near perfection as a damsel could reach, but he could not help acknowledging that Lettice Audley was her superior.

Mistress Audley was anxious to hear Captain Layton's opinion and what plans he proposed. "He is, indeed, a true, generous friend," she exclaimed, when Roger told her that his father had actually purchased a stout ship in which he was about to sail in the hopes of recovering her husband.

"But the first thing we have to do is to ascertain, more exactly than we now know, the part of the country to which he has been carried," observed Roger. "I therefore propose setting off at once to London, to learn, from those with whom the seaman Richard Batten returned, the place where they received him on board; and then, with your leave, Mistress Audley, I will come back here to make our final arrangements. Do you yourself propose accompanying your sons? or will you remain here with your daughter till we have concluded our search, and returned, as I hope, successful?"

"I cannot so far restrain my anxiety as to remain at a distance while others are engaged in the search, and if a way is opened out to us, my daughter Lettice and I have resolved to proceed to Virginia," answered Mistress Audley.

"You are a brave lady, truly," exclaimed Roger; "my sister Cicely purposes going for the sake of being with our father, and it would be an honour and satisfaction if you would take a passage on board his ship."

Mistress Audley expressed her gratitude, and said she would consult her son Vaughan on the subject.

Roger Layton did not attempt to conceal the admiration he felt for Lettice Audley, and he would gladly have remained another day could he have found sufficient excuse. Duty had, however, always been his guiding star, and he accordingly the next morning at daybreak was ready to depart. He had taken leave of Mistress Audley and Lettice the night before, but when the morning came Lettice was in the parlour to serve him with breakfast, and he enjoyed some minutes of her society before her brothers made their appearance. They came down booted and spurred, prepared to accompany him part of the way. He promised not to spare his good steed; but even so, he could not hope to be back much within a fortnight, and soon after that time he expected that the *Rainbow* would be ready for sea, and he thus could not remain more than a day at Mistress Audley's on his way to Plymouth.

In the evening Vaughan and Gilbert returned home. As they reached the gate, they were surprised to see two stout horses, held by a groom, standing before it. They inquired who had arrived. " Your worships' cousin, master Harry Rolfe and a stranger, a stout and comely gentleman, who has the air and speech of a sea-captain—though he may be, judging by his looks, some great lord," answered the groom.

" Poor Harry ! I thought after the unkind treatment as he called it which he received from our sister, that he would not come back again to this house—but I shall be glad to see him," observed Vaughan to his brother.

As they entered the parlour, they found their mother and Lettice with the two gentlemen who had just arrived. Their cousin, Harry Rolfe, whose appearance was much in his favour, sprang from his seat to greet them, and introduced his companion as Captain John Smith, " With whom, in the company of many other right worshipful gentlemen, I am about to sail for Virginia," he added. " I could not quit England without coming to bid you farewell : for it may be my lot, as it has been that of many others, not to return."

Mistress Audley sighed as he spoke. " Pardon me, kind aunt, for the inadvertence of my expression," he exclaimed.

" You are thinking of our father," said Gilbert ; " but we have had news that he is still alive, and you will, I know, gladly join us in searching for him."

Captain Smith on this made inquiries regarding the subject of which they were speaking, and such information as they possessed was given him. He listened attentively, and promised to use all the means in his power in searching for Captain Audley. His words greatly raised Mistress Audley's spirits ; for he was evidently a man who would carry out whatever he purposed. Already advancing towards middle life, he possessed an eagle eye, a determined expression of countenance, and a strongly-knit figure capable of enduring fatigue and hardship.

Harry Rolfe further informed his relations that he and Captain Smith were on their way to join their ship, the *Hector*, at Plymouth, into which port she and several others were to put before proceeding on their voyage. The countenance of Harry Rolfe brightened as he heard that his relatives purposed proceeding to Virginia; but Lettice turning away her head as he expressed his pleasure at the thoughts of their coming, he looked disappointed and grieved. Mistress Audley, as in courtesy bound, invited her visitors to remain to supper; but they excused themselves on the plea that they must hasten on in case their ship should arrive at Plymouth, and expected to sleep some ten miles further on their road. Taking their leave, therefore, they proceeded on their journey.

Mistress Audley was naturally agitated with many doubts and fears as to the propriety of proceeding. She herself was ready to encounter any dangers or hardships for the purpose of encouraging the search for her husband, and for the sake of sooner meeting him, but she doubted whether it was right to expose her young daughter Lettice to such risk; while her eldest son, though without him she could not proceed, would be drawn away from his studies at Cambridge and from the career he had chosen; but her children were unanimous in their desire to go to Virginia, and Lettice declared that even without such a motive she would willingly undertake the voyage.

She had a near neighbour, Captain Massey White, once Governor so called of Virginia, though there had been few men to govern, and those very ungovernable. He was now advanced in life and broken in health. Him she consulted : he spoke cautiously. If the new adventurers acted wisely they might succeed. The country was of exceeding richness, and the natives, though savage, might be won over. He could not advise a wife against seeking her husband, though many dangers must be encountered. To him the subject brought sad recollection. His only daughter and her husband, Ananias Dane, with their infant, a little girl, had been slaughtered with many others by the Indians, their only other child, their son Oliver, happily escaping, having been left with his grandame in England when they went to the colony. Oliver Dane, a boy of spirit and intelligence some years younger than Gilbert, was a frequent visitor at the house of Mistress Audley and a great favourite of hers. She pitied him also, for his grandfather could but ill manage him or afford him the amusements suited to his age. He, like many boys of those days, was longing to go to sea—to visit strange countries, and to engage in the adventures of which he often heard from the mariners he met with in Dartmouth. The result of her conversation with Captain White strengthened the resolution of Mistress Audley to proceed to Virginia. When young Dane heard of it, he was mad to go also. He begged Vaughan, who had a great liking for the lad, to take him. He had no need to ask

Gilbert, who declared that they would not leave him behind.

Mistress Audley and Lettice were pleased at the thoughts of having him with them.

Strange to say, the old man was willing to part with him. He must ere long go into the world to seek his fortune, and he could not be placed under better superintendence than that of Vaughan Audley, for whom he had a high esteem, and who would afford him instruction and watch over his interests. It was thus settled, to the great delight of Oliver Dane, after much more had been said than need be repeated, that he should accompany Mistress Audley and her family to Virginia.

Such of their goods as they considered likely to be of use, were packed up in fitting packages for stowage on board ship, and such other arrangements for the disposal of their property as were deemed necessary were made with the help of a trustworthy lawyer at Dartmouth. Seeing that the task was new to all of them, it was only just accomplished when Roger Layton arrived from London, accompanied by two men, Ben Tarbox and Nicholas Flowers by name, who had belonged to the *Sally Rose*, in which Richard Batten had escaped from Virginia. They were both willing to return to the country, and gave so circumstantial an account of the part they had visited, and were so certain that they could find their way to it again, that Roger had no doubt about the matter. Vaughan, who examined them much as a lawyer would a witness, was well satisfied on that

score, but not so in other respects with one of
the men, Nicholas Flowers, whom he set down in
his mind from the first as an arrant rogue. Of Ben
Tarbox Vaughan formed a better opinion, that he
was an honest fellow, with a fair amount of wits.

Roger brought also a letter from Sir George
Summers, to whom he had been introduced in London,
and who had known and esteemed Captain Audley,
offering to give a passage to Mistress Audley and
her family on board the *Sea Venture,* which ship
was about to sail from the Thames, and to come
round to Plymouth, where she was to be joined by
seven others, so the letter stated, though their names
were not mentioned. Sir George was most kind
and pressing; for the regard he bore her husband,
he assured Mistress Audley that she should be put
to no expense, and as the ship was large and well-
found, she might hope to have a prosperous voyage,
with fewer discomforts than are the lot generally
of those who tempt the dangers of the sea.

" For Sir George's offer we should indeed be
thankful," observed Mistress Audley, when she came
to the end of the letter ; " it seems like the guiding
of Providence, and we are in duty bound not to
refuse it."

To this Roger could raise no objection, though he
confessed that he was disappointed at not having
Mistress Audley and her daughter as passengers on
board the *Rainbow.* They would, however, sail
in company, and in calm weather he might hope to
pay them a visit, and at all events they would meet

at the end of their voyage. Roger found a letter waiting him from his father, stating that the *Rainbow* was nearly ready for sea, and advising that Mistress Audley and her family should come round by water from Dartmouth, as the easiest means of transporting their goods. Roger was glad of this opportunity of remaining longer in the company of Mistress Lettice, and of offering that assistance which his experience enabled him to give. He at once hastened to Dartmouth, where he engaged a pinnace with eight rowers, the master of which undertook, the sea being calm, to carry them to Plymouth between sunrise and sunset.

There were many tears shed by those on whom Mistress Audley and Lettice had bestowed kindness, as they set out from the home they were leaving, probably for ever, mounted on pillions; the pack-horses with their goods following in a long line. Mistress Audley rode behind Vaughan, and Lettice sat on the horse with her younger brother, beside whom rode Roger Layton, while Oliver Dane on his grandfather's nag—seldom now bestrode by the old man—trotted up now to one party, now to the other, but found Vaughan more ready to talk than was Roger, who had ears only for what Mistress Lettice might please to say. Thus they proceeded till they reached Dartmouth, close to which lay the pinnace Roger had hired. The goods were placed on board that evening, that they might sail without hindrance at dawn on the following morning.

The calm harbour lay in deepest shade, although

the summits of the rocks on the western side were
already tinged with the rays of the rising sun, as the
pinnace, propelled by eight stout rowers, glided out
towards the blue sea, rippled over by a gentle breeze
from the eastward.   The pinnace coasted along the
rocky shore till the long, low point of the Start was
rounded, when, altering her course, she steered for
Plymouth Sound, keeping well inside that fearful
rock, the Eddystone, on which many a bark has left
her shattered ribs.   Roger talked much to Lettice
as he sat by her side.   He told her of the voyages
he had made, of his last ship, when their brave pilot,
that renowned navigator, John Davis, with many of
his followers, was treacherously slain by the crew of

a Chinese ship they had captured,—Roger himself, with a few fighting desperately, having alone regained their boat as the Chinaman, bursting into flame, blew up, all on board perishing. Lettice gasped for breath as she listened to the tale; then Roger changed the subject and told her of the wonderful islands of the East, with their spice-groves and fragrant flowers; of the curious tea-plant; of the rich dresses of the natives; of the beautiful carved work and ornaments of all sorts which he had brought home.

" I have had them placed in my father's house, and they will please you to look at, Mistress Lettice," he observed; " for it may be some days before the fleet sails, and as my father could not bring himself to part with his house, it will afford you a home while you remain at Plymouth."

Gilbert and Oliver Dane were interested listeners to Roger's tales, though the descriptions of battles fought and hair-breadth escapes produced a very different effect in them; while she trembled and turned pale, they only longed to have been with Roger, and looked forward to the opportunity some day of imitating him.

Both wind and tide had favoured the voyagers, and before sunset the pinnace lay at anchor directly in front of Captain Layton's house. The captain had seen them coming, and with Cicely beside him was on the shore to welcome them. With becoming gallantry he pressed Mistress Audley's hand to his lips, while he bestowed a kiss on Lettice's fair brow, telling her how glad he was to greet her father's daughter. Cicely then took her hand, and led her towards the house, while the captain assisted Mistress Audley up the steep ascent.

The captain having well calculated the time they would arrive, a handsome repast was already laid in the hall, to which the superior officers of the *Rainbow*, and some of those of gentle birth intending to go passengers by her, were invited. Three of the other vessels destined to form the fleet had arrived, but the admiral's ship, the *Sea Venture*, had not yet come round from the Thames. The time was spent by the young people with much satisfaction to themselves, and so well pleased was Mistress Audley with Cicely that when Vaughan told her that he wished to make her his wife, she did not object to his pledging his troth, though she warned him that the present was not a time to take upon himself the cares of a wife and family, and that all his thoughts must be employed in the sacred duty in which he was engaged.

At length a tall ship was seen sailing up the harbour with gay flags flying from the mastheads. The other vessels as she approached saluted her with their guns; the captain, who was on the watch, pronounced her to be the *Sea Venture*, the ship of the good admiral, Sir George Summers, commanded by Captain Newport, with Sir Thomas Gates, the new Governor of Virginia, on board. Soon after she dropped anchor the admiral's barge was seen leaving the ship, and Captain Layton went down to beg that he would remain at his house till the fleet was ready to sail. Sir George, whose shipmate he had formerly been, was well pleased to accept his offer; Mistress Audley had thus an early opportunity of thanking the admiral for his generous offer.

" The thanks are due from me, Mistress Audley, that you condescend to take passage with your family on board my ship," he answered, with proper gallantry.

Mistress Audley told Sir George of Captain Layton's desire that she should sail on board his ship. " I will not act the hypocrite, and say that I am sorry to deprive him of the pleasure," answered Sir George, " and having gained your promise to sail on board my ship, I intend to keep you to it."

Sir George was accompanied by several cabin boys, one of whom he brought on shore, and introduced as the son of his old friend, that brave sea-captain and good knight, Sir Edward Fenton, lately deceased. Ned Fenton, who was now going for his first voyage, and Gilbert soon became fast friends, and were well pleased to find that they were to continue together. The remainder of the passengers of the fleet now arrived, most of whom were gentlemen of good family, though of broken fortunes—a class ill fitted for the work before them ; while the remainder were artisans far more likely to succeed than the former in a new colony.

At length the whole of the fleet to which the

Rainbow was joined gathered in the Sound, and a brave appearance they presented as seen from the windows of the captain's house, their flags flying and their sails hanging in the brails ready to sheet home as soon as the admiral should give the signal to weigh anchor. The wind, however, continued blowing from the westward, and eager as they were to depart, the admiral knew that it would be useless to proceed to sea when no progress could be made towards their destination.

Gilbert and Oliver spent most of their time on board the *Sea Venture*, to which, through the kindness of Sir George Summers, they had been appointed as officers, that they might receive wages from the company; but Vaughan, who had no fancy for a sea-life, found ample occupation on shore in attending on Mistress Cicely, while she had no objection to be so attended. She consenting to his proposal of marriage, he had spoken to her father. " I would not desire a more worthy son-in-law," answered the captain ; " but she and you are young, and can afford to wait till we have founded our new settlement, and have houses to dwell in, and lands we can call our own to cultivate. You may deem me unkind ; but I were more unkind to grant your request, judging as I do what is best for you both. A sea voyage, even though you are in different ships, will not cool your love, and if, as I am sure will be the case, some months hence you are of the same mind, your mother and, as I hope, your father also agreeing thereto, I will no longer prohibit your marriage."

Thus Vaughan and Cicely, as many other young people have had to do, had to wait patiently, looking forward with hope to the future.

CHAPTER III.

T length a gun was fired from the admiral's ship,—the signal for the fleet to weigh anchor. It was at once repeated by a whole salvo from Captain Layton's battery, discharged according to the captain's directions by Barnaby, who had been left as guardian of the house and property, the owner deeming it possible that he might some day return to his own home. The wind had veered round to the north-east, and blew a fresh breeze, which it was hoped would speedily waft them across the ocean. The *Sea Venture* took the lead, the *Rainbow* following close astern, and the other vessels in their different order of sailing. Thus the fleet glided on. The blue Lizard, growing dimmer and dimmer, sank beneath the ocean; the Land's End was lost to sight, and the fleet, guided by the wondrous compass, sped onward, chasing the sun in its course. For several days the wind continued fair, the ocean calm, and all on board looked forward to a speedy termination of their voyage. Audley watched with interest the *Rainbow* as she kept her course, sometimes drawing close enough to enable him to see Mistress Cicely on her deck. It is possible that her young mate

might have done his best, by pressing on sail, to keep her there, in order that he himself might have the satisfaction of seeing Mistress Lettice, with her mother and other ladies seated on the high poop of the admiral's ship, under an awning spread to shelter them; for the wind being light and aft, the sun beat down with no slight force, and few would willingly have remained long exposed to its burning rays. The sea, just crisped over with wavelets, glittered brightly, and ever and anon huge fish rose to the surface and gambolled round the ships, wondering what strange monsters had come to invade their watery domain. Gilbert, Oliver, and Fenton were in the mean time busying themselves about their duties. Gilbert had undertaken to instruct his younger companions in such nautical knowledge as he possessed: Ned was an apt pupil, and he hoped to do no discredit to the name of his honoured father.

" I had expected on coming to sea to meet the huge waves towering as high as the mastheads, and strong winds, and thunder and lightning; but the life we lead in this calm weather is so pleasant and easy that I should soon grow weary of it," observed Fenton.

" Wait a bit," answered Gilbert; " my experience is not very great, but I can tell you that the ocean is not always in its present humour, and that we may have another account to give before we reach the shores of Virginia."

Still the fine weather continued; and at length so completely did the wind fall that the ships lay rolling

their sides slowly to and fro, their tall masts reflected
in the mirror-like ocean, it being necessary even for
the boats to be lowered to keep them apart. The
opportunity was taken by many to visit each other's
ships. Vaughan went with his brother on board the
Rainbow, and Mistress Cicely welcomed him in a
way which made him wish that he might continue
the voyage with her; but he remembered that his
mother and sister were on board the *Sea Venture,*
and that duty required him to be with them, that,
should any mishap occur, he might be at his post to
protect them as far as he had the power. Roger
Layton received a similar welcome from Lettice;
although he had not spoken to her, she was perfectly
well acquainted with the state of his heart, and
knowing that he was equally well acquainted with
hers, she remained satisfied that God would order
all for the best. Mistress Audley was well pleased
with the young sailor; she had discerned his good
qualities, and the wealth he would inherit from his
father was sufficient for the position in life she desired for her daughter. There is an old saying that
" the course of true love never did run smooth ";
in this instance it seemed, however, that the proverb
was not to prove a correct one.

As darkness was coming on, the admiral ordered
the boats to return to their respective ships, and
the lights in the lanterns on the stern of the *Sea
Venture* were kindled for the guidance of the fleet
at night. Towards morning there was a change in
the weather. Dark clouds were chasing each other

rapidly across the sky; the sea, of a leaden hue, tossed and tumbled with foaming crests; the seamen were busy aloft furling sails, and the ships, which had hitherto kept close together, now, for safety's sake, separated widely. The wind whistled in the shrouds; the waves dashed against the lofty sides of the *Sea Venture*, whose fortunes we must now follow. Still the stout ship kept her course, under reduced canvas.

" I told you, Ned, that it was not always calm and sunshine," observed Gilbert, while he and his friends clung to the weather-bulwarks as the ship plunged into the heavy seas. " I wonder how the other ships are faring? Let us climb into the main-rigging and see."

Fenton, Oliver, and he did as proposed, and holding on to the shrouds they gazed over the storm-tossed ocean. Every instant the wind was increasing in strength, and the waves in height, amid which the other ships were seen tossing and tumbling, thrown, as it were from sea to sea, with but a small amount of canvas to steady them, and even then it seemed as much as they could bear.

" I wonder which is the *Rainbow*," continued Gilbert; " Vaughan and Lettice will be watching her with no small anxiety. See, there they stand on the poop-deck, straining their eyes towards the ship they suppose to be her : truly, I should grieve were any misfortune to happen to those on board."

" So should I," said Fenton; " but it is a hard matter to make out which is the *Rainbow*, though

E

I thought that I could distinguish her from the rest."

Every moment the gale increased, and the seas rose higher and higher ; six strong men were at the helm, but even then with difficulty could the ship be steered. The sails were closely furled, with the exception of a small foretopsail, and away the stout ship flew—now dipping into one sea, the foaming crest of which came rushing over the deck, now rising to the summit of another. Still Lettice, with her brother's arm round her waist to secure her, stood on the poop ; her face was pale, though not with alarm for herself or those with her so much as for the *Rainbow*, for she naturally thought " if such is the buffeting our large ship is receiving, what must be the condition of so small a bark as the *Rainbow,*" towards which ship her and her brother's eyes were cast, as they supposed. Those who could have distinguished one ship from the other were busy in attending to their respective duties.

Gilbert and his messmates still kept their post ; they, too, were watching, as they believed, the *Rainbow*, which was endeavouring, as it seemed, to set more canvas, to bear up for the Admiral. Now she appeared sinking into the deep trough of the sea, now tossed up helplessly to the summit of another, again to descend, when her hull could scarcely be distinguished amid the masses of foam which danced madly round her. As she lay deep down in the watery valley a huge sea rolled over her deck, and she did not rise again on the other side.

A cry escaped from the three lads: "She's gone! she's gone!"—echoed by many on deck.

Lettice, with straining eyes, gazed at the spot where the ship had been. Vaughan, his heart torn with anguish, endeavoured to support her, but could ill restrain his own feelings, believing as he did that Cicely had perished. The admiral had seen what had occurred, and with gentle force conveyed her to the cabin, where she could receive from her mother that comfort she needed so much; while the governor with friendly sympathy, taking Vaughan's arm, endeavoured to calm his agitation and prevent him from madly leaping into the sea.

" Oh, steer the ship to their assistance! We must go and help them," shouted Vaughan, not knowing what he said.

" The attempt were vain," said the captain; " long ere we could reach the spot where yonder ship has gone down, all who were on board her will have perished "; and he made a sign to the governor, and others standing round to carry the young man below. They succeeded, Vaughan moving like one in a dream. The admiral assured Lettice and her brother that it was possible the ship they had seen go down was not the *Rainbow*, for though small compared to their own ship, she was a stout, well-built bark, and might contend successfully with even a worse storm than was then blowing; adding that one of the vessels seen in the distance bore a great resemblance to her; indeed, by every means in his power, he endeavoured to restore their spirits. He was compelled, however, soon to leave them, to attend to the navigation of the ship. He and Captain Newport held an earnest consultation, for the fierce storm, instead of giving signs of abating, was hourly gaining strength.

The wind, which first came from the north-east, now shifted suddenly round, greatly increasing the height of the seas, and fearfully straining the labouring vessel.

Night coming on, the other ships were lost to sight; no one could tell in what direction they had gone. Those who were inclined to look at matters in the darkest light believed that they had foundered. Not for a moment did the brave admiral leave the deck. Now, the rain pouring down, all was pitchy darkness; and then suddenly a vivid flash of lightning showed the whole deck, and the pallid faces of the crew—for even the stoutest-hearted looked pale; and well they might, for the raging seas threatened every instant to engulf them. Few men surrounded by such horrors can face death unappalled.

Thus that dreadful night passed on. But matters had not come to the worst; the admiral sat on the deck, conning the ship, endeavouring with all the nautical skill he possessed, in which no man surpassed him, to keep her before the wind. The carpenter, who had been below to sound the well, rushed up, a flash of lightning exhibiting his countenance pale as death. "We've sprung a fearful leak, sir," he exclaimed; "it's my belief that the oakum is washed out of the seams, for already the water is rising above the ballast."

" Then hasten with your crew, search out where the worst leaks exist, and strive to stop them," said the admiral, calmly; "man the pumps, and let others be told off with buckets to bale out the water. We must not give way to despair; often have men been in a worse condition on board ship, and by persevering efforts have preserved their lives."

The determined way in which the admiral spoke somewhat restored the confidence of the crew ; some with lanterns in their hands crept into the wings on either side of the ship, close to the ribs, searching every corner, and listening attentively to discover the place where the water entered. Others, like galley-slaves, stripped to the waist, went to the pumps, and worked away with that desperate energy which men exhibit when they believe that their lives depend on the efforts they are making. Several of the leaks were found, but still the water came rushing in on all sides. The carpenter again reported that it was still rising, and, from the quantities of bread brought up, that the chief leak must be in the bread-room. Here he once more made search, but failed to discover the spot at which the water entered. The officers of all ranks exerting themselves to the ut-most, the men followed their example, while the passengers offered to labour with them. Vaughan Audley found the task he, with others, had undertaken, a great relief to his grief and anxiety ; with Gilbert

and young Fenton, he was working now away at the pumps; now he was standing one of the line formed to pass the buckets up from below. Even the women desired to take their share in the work. All on board were divided into three parties —while one party laboured at the pumps, or passed up the buckets for an hour at a time, the others, exhausted by their exertions, lay down to rest. An officer stood ready to give the signal as soon as the time arrived for the working party to be relieved.

Daylight at length returned, but showed no improvement in the weather; the wind blew as furiously as ever. Not for a moment had the brave admiral left his post. Just before noon a prodigious sea came rolling towards the ship, and, breaking over her bow, washed fore and aft, filling her from the hatches up to the spar-deck. For some time it appeared impossible that she could shake herself clear of the mass of water, which, as it rushed aft, dashed the men from the helm, forcing the tiller out of their hands, and tossed them helplessly from side to side. It seemed a wonder that none were carried overboard or received mortal injury. The admiral, too, was thrown from his seat and, as were several officers round him, cast with his face on the deck. Still, while endeavouring to recover himself, he shouted to others of the crew, who flew to the helm and prevented the ship from broaching to. Though she was running at the time under bare poles at the rate of scarcely less than eight knots an hour, for a moment the violence of the shock stopped her way, and many thinking that she had struck on a rock, shouted out, " We are lost ! we are lost ! "

" Not yet, my brave fellows," cried the admiral; " while there is life there is hope! The ship is still swimming : all hands to their stations."

Another voice was heard clear and clarion-toned amid the howling of the storm, as the voices of God's ministers should sound at all times:—"Turn to Him who calmed the tempest on the sea of Galilee. Why are ye affrighted, oh ye of little faith? Trust to Him all powerful to save, not your frail bodies only from the perils of the deep, but your immortal souls from just condemnation. Turn ye, turn ye! why will ye die? He calls to you ; He beseeches you. Trust to Him! trust to Him ! "

He who spoke was the good chaplain, Master Hunt, who had been ceaselessly supporting the sorely-tried ones below with words of comfort from the

book of life, and who had now come on deck to perform his duty to the fainting crew.

The men, thus encouraged, returned to their duty,
and worked away with the same vigour as before.
Even during this fearful time neither Vaughan nor
Gilbert had quitted the pump at which they were
labouring. Though Vaughan, believing that Cicely
was lost, cared little for life, yet he thought of his
mother and sister, and felt that it was his duty at all
events to labour for their sakes.

" Don't give way, brother," cried Gilbert, " our
mother has often said that God watches over us, and
if it is His good will He can preserve us even now.
The carpenter has just stopped another leak, and I
heard him say that he hoped the rest might be got
at. We may be thankful that we have strength to
work."

"Spell, oh ! " was soon after this cried, and a fresh
party hurrying from the cabins and from the more
sheltered spots where they had thrown themselves
down to rest, came to relieve those who had been
working for the last hour. Thus two days went by,
but the storm abated not; no land was in sight ; few
indeed on board knew whither they were driving ;
all they could do was to labour on, and then to lie
down in order to gain fresh strength for renewed
labours. Sometimes the wind came from the north;
then shifted to the north-east, often in an instant
veering two or three points, and almost half round
the compass. The brave admiral did his best to
steer west by south, but that was no easy matter.

In spite of all on board, as the water was still increasing, he gave orders to lighten the ship by throwing overboard numerous casks of beer, oil, cider and wine, which to those who loved their liquor was sadly trying; but just then life to them was dearer than aught else. The hold being filled, scarcely any fresh water or beer could be got at, nor could a fire be lighted in the cook-room to dress their meat. Thus, thirsty and famished, the crew had to toil from day to day, while such refreshment as sleep could have afforded was well-nigh denied them.

All this time three pumps were kept working, and not for a moment did they cease baling out with their buckets, baricos, and kettles. Still, notwithstanding their utmost exertions, the ship had now ten feet of water in her hold, and had they for a single watch ceased to pump, she must have foundered. At length the admiral gave the order to heave overboard the guns; it was a desperate remedy, for should the ship survive the gale and an enemy be met with, she must helplessly yield; a greater trial to her brave crew than any they had encountered. One after one, the tackles cast off, the guns were sent plunging into the ocean. Relieved of their weight, the ship floated somewhat more buoyantly.

"We have done our best," exclaimed the brave admiral. "One more resource remains to us, we must cut away the masts."

All knew that this was indeed a desperate remedy, for the huge ship would thus float a mere log on the water, waiting if, by God's good providence, some other vessel might bear down to their relief. But of that there was little prospect; still their lives might thus be prolonged a few short hours, and true men know that it is their duty to struggle to the last, and trust to God for their preservation.

All this time no observation had been taken, for neither was the sun to be seen by day, nor the stars by night. Gilbert and Fenton, with young Oliver, had after their exertions turned in for a short time: even the howling of the tempest, the dashing of the waves, and the terrible condition of the shattered ship did not prevent them from sleeping. Summoned by the boatswain's hoarse cry, they again hastened on deck to attend to their duty. The admiral was there, and as they were standing near him, they saw him gaze up at the main-mast head.

" Gilbert, Gilbert, what can that be ? " exclaimed Oliver.

Gilbert looked in the direction his messmate pointed, and there he saw a small round light, like a faint tremulous star, streaming along and sparkling brightly, now bursting into a blaze, now resuming its round form ; sometimes running up and down the shrouds, now along the main-yard to the very end, there remaining for an instant, and then returning as if about to settle on the mast-head, then again descending once more to perform the same journey as before. The eyes of all on deck were directed towards it; some exclaimed that it was the demon of the storm come to warn them that their minutes were numbered.

"My friends," cried the admiral, "if it were an evil spirit it would not come to warn men to prepare for death. To my mind it is of the same nature as the lightning, but harmless. Several times before have I seen it, and on each occasion the storm has shortly after broken. If sent for any purpose, it is to encourage us to persevere, and to assure us that ere long the wind will abate, and we shall gain the mastery over our ship. To the pumps, my friends, to the pumps! and keep the buckets moving."

The admiral's brave words restored new life to the well-nigh exhausted crew; once more the pumps were worked vigorously, and the buckets were passed rapidly from below. At dawn the admiral himself was seen ascending the rigging. For a few minutes he remained at the masthead; then he waved his hat, and shouted, "Land! land!" At that joyful cry many who had fallen asleep in the cabins or other sheltered parts of the ship, over-come with fatigue, were aroused, and hurrying on deck, gazed anxiously towards the shore on which they hoped to find that safety denied to them by the ocean. Again they went to the pumps, and once more set to work to bale with buckets, baricos, and kettles, endeavouring to keep the ship afloat till a place of safety should be reached.

The admiral remained still longer watching the distant shore, towards which he ordered the ship to be steered. As she approached, numerous small islands were seen ahead: the sight revived the spirits of all on board. The leadsman was ordered to sound as the ship ran on; first thirteen fathoms of water were found, then seven. Some spoke of anchoring, but the admiral, though he would gladly have saved the ship, knew full well that she would not float many hours longer. Again he ascended the mast, and looking out saw a spot between two high rocks, towards which he ordered the helmsman to steer. The foresail only was set, to prevent the ship from striking with too great force. The passengers and crew were collected on deck; still to the last the pumps were kept going, and the buckets were worked, lest she might founder even before she could reach the shore. It was now known that they had arrived at the stormy Bermoothes, or as some call them the " Devil's Islands," owing to the fearful storms which rage round them, and the numerous dangers they present to navigators.

Islands, many hundreds in number, extended three or four leagues on either side of the one towards which the ship's course was directed. Trees could now be discerned on it waving to and fro in the wind: but as the ship sped on the force of the waves decreased, and as she gradually got under the shelter of the islands, the water became sufficiently smooth to encourage the hope that she would not go to pieces when she should strike the shore. But then the crew asked each other were they about to be thrown on a desolate island, where neither food nor water could be found?"

The admiral had descried two high rocks at a short distance apart, near which the water seemed smoother than at any other part. He now directed the course of the ship towards it; not a moment was to be lost, for the water was rapidly rising higher and higher in the hold. He warned those on deck to beware, lest the ship striking suddenly, the masts might fall and crush those below them. Vaughan on this led Mistress Audley and his sister back into the cabin, but Gilbert declared that as an officer he must run the risk of whatever might happen. All waited with suspense for the expected shock; the minutes seemed hours; every instant the objects on shore became more and more distinct —the rocks, the beach, the trees beyond, and here and there gentle slopes; but no mountains, or even hills worthy of the name.

Vaughan endeavoured to encourage his mother and Lettice, as well as the other ladies and children. Presently there came a grating sound, but the ship glided on till she finally stopped, and then there came a shout, "We are safe! we are safe!" Vaughan, on rushing on deck found that the ship had glided on to a sandbank, while the shore of an island appeared little more than half a mile away, offering an easy landing to the storm-tossed voyagers. Thanksgivings arose from many a heart on board for their preservation; but others, it must be owned, thought only how they might most quickly get on shore.

The admiral forthwith ordered the boats to be lowered, directing Captain Newport to summon those by name who were to go in them. The governor, as was right, went in the first, with all the women and children. As no signs of natives had been seen, it was not feared that opposition would be met with; nevertheless, the smaller boats were sent first to pilot the way. Vaughan and two other gentlemen passengers were requested to accompany the governor, in order to assist in taking care of the ladies. They were watched with some anxiety as they took their departure.

The passage to the shore was accomplished without difficulty, and the boats entered a beautiful little bay, with a sandy beach, where the passengers easily landed. "Let us return thanks to Heaven for our preservation," exclaimed the good chaplain, as they stepped on shore; when all kneeling down, led by one who prayed not only with the lips but with his whole heart, they lifted up their voices to Him to whose mighty arm they gratefully acknowledged their preservation alone was due. The boats being immediately sent back to the ship, in a few trips the whole of those on board were landed. As there was still sufficient daylight, the boats were then again despatched to bring away provisions, as well as the carpenter's tools and other articles of the greatest necessity, including some sails for tents, that the ladies and the governor and the other older persons might have shelter for the night. The rest, by cutting down branches, made huts for themselves, with beds of leaves; and thus, as soon as supper had been taken—the first quiet meal they had enjoyed since the storm began—the whole of the worn-out crew and passengers lay down to sleep, with the exception of those told off to keep watch. Probably, ere many minutes were over, the weary sentries also closed their eyes. But a God of mercy watched over the shipwrecked company, and no harm befell them.

The next morning being calm and beautiful, the boats were sent off to bring more provisions and other articles which could be saved from the wreck. Thus they were employed all day, while those who remained on shore, when not unloading the boats, were engaged in erecting huts. A day of toil was succeeded by another night of rest; all worked willingly under the able directions of the governor, the admiral, and Captain Newport. To assist in the more rapid landing of the cargo, a raft was constructed, and in a short time everything the ship contained was taken out of her. This being done, she was completely unrigged, when the sails and ropes and spars were landed. They then proceeded to pull the ship herself to pieces for the purpose of building another vessel in which to continue the voyage to Virginia, should no assistance be sent from thence in the mean time to them. It was a task of great labour, but the admiral setting the example, and working himself as hard as any of the men, the others were fain to labour also. Gilbert, young Dane, and Fenton acted as his assistants, and were proud of the praises he bestowed upon them for their diligence and perseverance. Vaughan worked as hard on shore, assisting the governor, who superintended the erection of the storehouse, and the huts in which all might find shelter ; and in a short time a village sprang up.

The ladies were not idle, doing their best to fit up their own houses and those of their friends. Under other circumstances Lettice and Vaughan would have been contented and happy; but the dreadful thought that the *Rainbow* had been lost, in spite of the assurances of the admiral, constantly occurred to them. Mistress Audley did her best to comfort her daughter, but the rose left Lettice's cheek, though she sought for strength to support her sorrow, whence strength alone can be obtained.

CHAPTER IV.

THE shipwrecked party were now settled in safety on the island. They had reason to be thankful that they had escaped the fearful perils of the sea; but they had no wish to remain where they were: Virginia was their destination, and thither they desired to proceed. They looked anxiously for the arrival of one of the ships of the squadron, which they hoped might be sent to search for them. No ship, however, made her appearance, and the indefatigable admiral accordingly set to work to improve the long-boat by raising the sides, and decking her over, and also by fitting her with masts and sails and oars.

In the mean time the officers turned their attention to the procuring of food for the settlement. Several seines had been brought in the ship; a sandy beach, free from rocks, afforded a favourable place for drawing them, though, as yet, they knew not what fish the sea would supply. The two small boats were brought round to the spot, and the seine was cast. With no slight eagerness, the greater number of the colonists stood on the shore, watch-

F

ing the success of the undertaking. The officers, as well as the men, assisted in drawing the net; as it approached the shore, the fins and tails of innumerable fish were seen splashing above the surface. Shouts of satisfaction rose from the spectators: the seamen, led by the admiral himself, rushed in, regardless of a wetting, to seize the fish, which were endeavouring to escape over the net, and fifty men or more were now floundering about, each grasping one or more of the struggling creatures. In their eagerness, several toppled over on their noses, and had to be picked up by their companions to be saved from drowning. Some came triumphantly to land, dragging huge fish, many pounds in weight, by the gills; several received severe bites from the sharp teeth of the fish, into whose mouths they had incautiously thrust their hands. Not a few scampered out, declaring that there were sharks or other monsters among the shoal, which had attacked their legs. Among the most eager were Gilbert, Fenton, and Oliver Dane. The three youths on all occasions bore each other company, and after each of them had secured a fish large enough to feed a dozen hungry men or more, Fenton and Oliver were seen coming out with an enormous one held fast by the gills, which, in consequence of its vehement struggles, they could with difficulty land. On the net being at length hauled up, enough fish were secured to feed the party for several days, besides those which had first been taken. Among them were numerous lobsters, crabs, and crawfish, which, it was conjectured, were the creatures the seamen had declared had bitten their legs. Here was an additional reason for thankfulness, for while the sea so plentifully supplied food, there need be no fear of hunger. In the holes of the rocks, salt in abundance was also found, with which the fish could be preserved, so as to afford provision at times when the tempestuous weather might prevent the seine being drawn. Still, fish alone would not be sufficient to feed the people, and parties were therefore sent out to search for such other food as nature might have provided. Vaughan with his brother, young Dane, and Fenton, honest Ben Tarbox, and two other men, formed one of the parties; the admiral, Captain Newport, and two of the lieutenants, leading others.

They had examined, as far as their eyes could serve them, the surrounding islands, but could see no smoke nor other signs of inhabitants; nor did they discover the slightest trace of wild beasts. From the masses of white foam which they saw breaking over the rocks in all directions, they rightly judged that reefs and shoals abounded, and that no ship could approach the group, except on the side on which they had providentially been cast.

Vaughan and Gilbert wished their mother and sister good-bye, promising to be back soon: they felt confident that they would be in no danger, while the governor remained to keep the rough seamen in order. As they walked along, great numbers of small birds, of various species, were met with. Oliver happened to be whistling while stopping to look about him, when, greatly to his surprise and that of his companions, a flock of small birds came down and alighted on the branches close to their heads.

"Stop," said Vaughan; "we must not frighten them, and see what they will do."

Oliver continued to whistle, holding out his hand, when half a dozen of the birds or more hopped off the branches and perched on his arm, looking up into his face, as if wondering whence the notes they heard proceeded. The rest of the party, imitating his example, and whistling loudly, several other flights of birds came round them, resting, without the slightest appearance of fear, on their heads and shoulders.

"'Twere a pity to abuse the confidence of the little feathered innocents," observed Vaughan, "though I fear much, before long, they will find out the treachery of man, and have to rue their simplicity."

"An it please you, sir, it is very likely, if we grow hungry," remarked Ben Tarbox; "but I for one wouldn't hurt them now, though I might be pretty sharp set."

"Keep to your resolve, my friend, and persuade your mates to be equally humane," said Vaughan.

As they moved on, the birds flew away to the surrounding trees, but followed them wherever they went. They had not got far, when Fenton, who was a little ahead, cried out, "A bear! a bear!" and immediately fired.

"I missed him," he exclaimed, as Vaughan and Gilbert joined him.

"I doubt much whether the animal you saw was a bear," said Vaughan, as they got up to the spot, examining the ground where Fenton declared he had seen the creature. "Observe these berries, and the way the soil has been turned up : a bear would have climbed the tree from which they have fallen; whereas, it is evident that an animal with a long snout has been feeding here. That tree is the palmetto, which, I have heard from those who have been in the West Indies, yields a cabbage most delicious to eat; these berries are also sweet and wholesome. By taking the trouble to climb to the summit, we may procure an ample supply of vege-tables; and see! there are many other trees of the same species. As we shall have no difficulty in finding them again, we will go on in search of the animal you saw; and, should our guns not prove faithless, we may hope to find some meat for dinner."

They now proceeded more cautiously, when, com-ing to the edge of an open glade, they saw before them a herd of thirty or more swine feeding at a short distance. Creeping along under shelter of the bushes, they got close enough to fire. Vaughan selected one animal, Gilbert and Fenton aimed at two others. Firing together, three hogs fell dead on the ground. Here was a prize worth ob-

taining; Tarbox and the other men, who understood cutting up a pig, were soon busily engaged
in the operation, while the gentlemen continued
their search farther on. Great was their delight to
discover pear-trees bearing ripe fruit, and at a little
distance a grove of mulberry-trees, some with
white, others with red fruit.

"In what a curious way the leaves are rolled
round," observed Gilbert, examining them; "why,
each contains a little conical ball, I verily believe,
of silk."

"Yes, indeed, they are silk-worms," said Vaughan; "there are enough here to supply the looms
of France for many a day; and if we can collect,
and can manage to unwind them, we may send home
a quantity certain to yield a rich return. We will
carry back a supply of the fruit, which will be
welcomed by our mother and sister."

Gilbert and his companions quickly wove a couple
of baskets of some long grass which grew near,
and filled them with mulberries and a few cocoons
of the silk-worms to exhibit to their friends. They
did not forget also to stuff their pockets full of
pears. Well pleased with the result of their excur-
sion, they returned to the settlement.

The admiral, who set an example of activity to
all the rest, undertook an expedition to visit the
neighbouring islands, giving leave to Gilbert and
Fenton to accompany him. As they pulled along,
they saw a number of birds flying towards a small
island. On landing, they discovered a vast number

of eggs, the size of hens' eggs, which had been laid upon the sand, the heat of which apparently assisted to hatch them. The birds were so tame that they allowed the men to come among them without moving, so that they could be knocked down with sticks. In a short time a thousand birds were caught, and as many eggs, so that the boat was loaded almost to her gunwale. Here was a further supply of welcome food, adding to the variety of that already obtained. One night, the boats returning from an expedition, the crews landed on an island to cook their supper, when, greatly to their surprise, they found themselves surrounded by birds which perched on their heads and arms, so as to almost cover them, many flying directly into the fire. Notwithstanding the shouts and laughter of the men, the birds came in still greater numbers, apparently attracted as much by the noise as the light, while they answered the shouts by a curious hooting; from which reason, and from their blindness, the men called them sea-owls. After this, the boats were frequently sent over, and by simply waving a firebrand, sea-fowls invariably collected round them, so that they in a short time could kill as many with their sticks as would fill the boats.

Not far off from the settlement was a sandy beach. Gilbert and his ever-constant companions were one evening returning homewards, when they caught sight of a creature crawling out of the sea. They hid themselves to watch what it would do; another and another followed, when, making their way up to a dry part of the beach, they were seen to stir up the sand, and to remain for some time at the spot. Vast numbers of others followed, and continued coming, till darkness prevented their being distingushed. Although neither of the lads had seen turtles, they guessed what they were, and, rushing out of their hiding-place, were quickly in their midst, endeavouring to catch some of them; but the creatures bit at their legs, and they, not knowing the art of turning them on their backs, were dragged along by those they caught hold of till they were nearly carried into the water. At length they gave up the attempt.

On their arrival at the settlement, they told what they had seen, when they were heartily laughed at for not having turned over the turtles. The next morning many of the men went out, and returned laden with turtles' eggs, which they had found in the sand. The following evening the turtles were not allowed much quiet, for the men, having armed themselves with long sticks, hid in the surrounding bushes, and as soon as the turtles had crawled on to the beach they set upon them, and before the frightened creatures could escape, some two score or more were turned on their backs, and in that condition were dragged to the settlement. It was on a Saturday night, and the next Sabbath morning good Master Hunt, the chaplain, failed not to remark on the kindness of Providence in thus supplying them so abundantly with wholesome food. The service being over, all the cooks, with many

assistants, making up the greater part of the inhabitants, were busy in dressing the turtle, some
making soup, others stews — indeed, of every mess
there was far more than the men, albeit large eaters
with voracious appetites, could consume.

Thus the settlement was amply supplied by Providence with all that people could desire. In truth,
it might have proved a perfect paradise, had not,
alas! the evil dispositions of the men broken out
to render it like other spots of this sinful earth.

The admiral finding that no ship arrived from
Virginia, despatched the long-boat under the command of Henry Raven, the master's mate, to that
settlement, a distance, as he calculated of a hundred and forty leagues. He promised, should he
arrive safely at his destination, to return immediately with a large vessel, capable of carrying all
the party. Many prayers were uttered for his safe
arrival and return, as he sailed away. Vaughan
did not fail to write to Captain Layton, as he also
did to Cicely; but, as he wrote, he stopped often
and groaned in spirit. Was she for whom these
lines were intended still alive to read them? "God
is good; God is merciful; He orders all things for
the best; His will be done," he said calmly. Then
he wrote on: he told of his deep anxiety, his agon-
izing fears; but he spoke also of his hopes, of his
trust in One all-powerful to save, of his eager
desire ere long to reach Virginia. Lettice likewise
wrote to her, giving many messages to Roger, to
whom she would fain herself have written, had the

so-doing been allowable. What she said need not
be repeated. It may be supposed that the long
separation the young people were doomed to endure was trying in the extreme. Mistress Audley
also felt great disappointment at being thus prevented from instituting the search for her husband,
though she confided in Captain Layton that he
would use all the means in his power to discover
his friend, had he, as she prayed, escaped ship-
wreck; and as she, with others, looked out day
by day for the arrival of the expected ship from
Virginia, she could not help believing that her
husband would be on board. She, like the rest, was
doomed to disappointment. Two moons went by
and no ship appeared. Had Master Raven arrived,
he would surely have returned by this time, and
fears were entertained that he and his compianons
must have been lost.

The keel of a pinnace had already been laid in
Gates's Bay, the name bestowed on the harbour on
the shore of which the settlement was situated.
Some progress had been made with her, when Sir
George Summers proposed going over to the chief
island, where there was an abundance of timber,
and taking with him two carpenters and a party of
men in order to build another vessel, it being evident that the first would not contain the whole of
the shipwrecked company. The governor willingly
agreed to the proposal, and Sir George and his
followers set off. The settlement was thus deprived
of many of the most trustworthy men.

Of many events which occurred on the island after this period we omit the account. Evil-disposed persons among the passengers and crew, forgetful of their merciful deliverance and of the supply of provisions afforded by their bountiful God to them, disregarding the exhortations of the chaplain, Master Hunt, to live peaceable lives, formed conspiracies against the governor and admiral with the intent of compassing their deaths. Happily, from want of union, these plots were discovered, but order was not restored until their ringleader had been seized and shot—a warning to the rest.

This state of things caused much alarm and anxiety to Mistress Audley and Lettice. Months passed by, the long-boat did not return. Had she arrived at the colony, they felt sure that, should the *Rainbow* have escaped, Captain Layton would have forthwith sailed in quest of them. Thus, to their minds it was clear that either the *Rainbow* or the long-boat had been lost. Happily for Mistress Layton and her children, they trusted in One mighty to save, who orders all for the best, and they could bow their heads in submission to His will, and say from their hearts, "Thy will be done."

While the admiral and his party were working away on the main island at the vessel he had undertaken to build, the governor and the carpenters who remained at Gates's Bay laboured on at the pinnace. Already great progress had been made with her ; oakum sufficient to caulk her was formed from old cables and ropes. One barrel of tar and another of pitch had also been saved. This however was not sufficient, and Vaughan, who had much scientific knowledge, invented a mixture composed of lime made of whelk shells and a hard white stone burned in a kiln, slaked with fresh water and tempered with tortoise-oil, with which she was payed over. She was built chiefly of cedar cut in the island, her beams and timbers being of oak saved from the wreck, and the planks of her bow of the same timber. She measured forty feet in the keel, and was nineteen feet broad; thus being of about eighty tons burden. She was named the *Deliverance*, as it was hoped that she would deliver the party from their present situation and carry them to the country to which they were bound.

The *Deliverance* was now launched, and found to sit well on the water. Shortly afterwards the pinnace built by Sir George Summers was seen coming round into the bay. She was smaller than the *Deliverance*, measuring nine-and-twenty feet in the keel, fifteen and a half in the beam, and drawing six feet water. Her name was the *Patience*, and truly with patience had she been built, the admiral having used such timber alone as he could cut in the forest, the only iron about her being a single bolt in the keelson. As no pitch or tar could be procured, she was payed over with a mixture of lime and oil, as was the *Deliverance*. All hands were now employed in fitting out the vessels and getting the stores on board.　At dawn on the 10th of May the admiral and captain put off in their long-boats to set buoys in the channel through which the vessels would have to pass, for the distance from the rocks to the shoals on the other side was often not more than three times the length of the ship.

A cross had been made by order of the governor of the wood of the wreck, having within it a coin with the king's head.　This cross was fixed to a great cedar tree in memory of their deliverance. To the tree was also nailed a copper plate with a fitting inscription.

About nine in the morning, the wind being fair, the whole of the company went on board.　The *Patience* led the way, with the admiral and those who had built her on board.　The *Deliverance*, in which Mistress Audley and her family were passengers, followed.

While all were in high spirits at finding themselves once more at sea, a severe blow was felt; the ship quivered from stem to stern, and a cry was raised, "We are on shore! we are on shore!" But the captain ordering the helm to be put up to larboard, and the starboard head-braces hauled aft and the after-sails clewed up, she glided on, carrying away a portion of the soft rock on which she had struck.　The well was sounded, but no leak was discovered, though for some time it was feared that, after the many months' labour bestowed on the ship, they might have to return.　For two days the vessels were threading the narrow channels amid those dangerous rocks, feeling, as it were, every inch of their way, with the dread each instant of striking.

Happily the weather remained calm, but even thus the time was one of great anxiety to all on board. At length, to their infinite joy, the captain announced that they were clear of all danger. The ship and pinnace shaped a course west and north to Virginia. Seven days after leaving the islands the colour of the water was seen to have changed, and branches of trees and other objects from the shore floated by. Sounding the next day, the ship was found to be in nineteen and a half fathoms of water. Lettice and Vaughan had remained late on deck, their hearts filled with anxiety, for on the morrow they might know whether those they loved were among the living or dead. Each tried to encourage the other, and as they stood watching the bright stars overhead and the calm ocean suffused with the silvery light of the moon, or gazing towards the land which they hoped ere long to see, they became sensible of a delicious odour of fruit and flowers wafted by the night breeze from the shore. The sails flapped against the masts, the vessel was taken aback, but the yards being braced round she stood on once more.

"To your cabin, Mistress Lettice, to your cabin," said Captain Newport, "we will, in God's good providence, take you in safely to-morrow; and now go to rest and dream of those you hope to meet, and the beautiful land to be your future home. Come, Master Audley, urge your sister to take my good advice."

Vaughan, knowing that the captain was right, led Lettice to the cabin.

CHAPTER V.

" LAND! land!" was shouted from the masthead just before the sun rose above the horizon, and Vaughan and Gilbert, with many others who hurried on deck, soon saw, just emerging from the ocean to the westward, two blue hummocks. In a short time the land was discerned, stretching away to the northward. The captain at once recognized the hummocks as landmarks to the southward of Chesapeake Bay, towards the mouth of which magnificent estuary the ship was now steered. The day was far advanced when they entered between two capes, since known as Cape Charles on the north and Cape Henry on the south of the bay, about twelve miles apart. Their destined harbour was still far away, and it was not till nearly two days more had passed that, early in the morning a small fort was seen about two miles south of Cape Comfort, at the entrance of James River. A gun was fired, and the English flag flying from the fort showed them that it was garrisoned by their friends. Captain Newport therefore sent a boat on shore to inform the commandant who they were.

While the vessels came to an anchor those on board eagerly looked out for the return of the boat, when they hoped that their many doubts and fears would be brought to an end. At length she came, bringing a stranger seated in the stern-sheets. The eyes of all on board were directed towards him. As the boat approached, he stood up and waved his hat, gazing eagerly at the ship.

"It is Roger Layton," shouted Gilbert, whose vision was one of the keenest of all on board.

"Yes, yes! it is he! it is he!" echoed Lettice, forgetting the presence of bystanders. The boat came alongside, and Roger sprang on deck; he, too, at first seemed not to recollect that there were others besides Lettice lookers-on, and, advancing towards her, he took her hand and pressed it to his lips, afterwards greeting Mistress Audley in the same manner.

"My father and sister are well," he answered to Audley's eager queries, as they warmly shook hands. He was quickly, however, plied with eager questions by many others, to which he could but briefly reply. The fleet had arrived safely, the ketch *Susan* excepted, which had foundered during the gale. The smaller vessels had gone up the river as far as James Town, where a settlement had been formed, and the larger, including the *Rainbow*, lay at anchor in Hampton Roads, whence he had come over to visit the commander of the fort. No great progress had been made in the settlement, for the commanders had disputed among themselves; the only true man among them being Captain Smith, who was the life and soul of the enterprise.

"And my husband, Captain Audley, have you gained any tidings of him?" asked Mistress Audley, in a trembling voice.

"Alas! Mistress Audley, we have not," answered Roger; "as yet we have had a hard matter to hold our own, surrounded as we have been by savages, whose friendship is doubtful. Notwithstanding this, our brave friend Captain Smith, Rolfe, and I, have made excursions in all directions, and, whenever we could, have communicated with the Indians, making inquiries for a white man residing among them. Even now, Captain Smith is away up the country, and he promised me that he would continue his inquiries. I, indeed, should have accompanied him, but my father is disheartened with the way affairs have been carried on, and poor Cicely is so much out of health that we were on the point of sailing for England. I trust that your arrival will cause him to change his plan, and you may depend on it that I will use my influence to induce him to do so."

"Of course you must," exclaimed Gilbert, "why, I have been looking forward to all sorts of adventures with you, and Vaughan there will greatly object to your going."

"Indeed shall I," said Vaughan, "and I propose, with your leave, going on shore with you, and proceeding overland to where the *Rainbow* is lying, concluding, as I do, that we shall get there sooner than the ship."

"You are right, and I shall be glad of your company," said Roger; "it will be the best proof to Cicely that you are not fathoms deep below the ocean, as she has been inclined of late to believe."

"What, has the long-boat with Master Raven not arrived?" asked Vaughan.

"We have had no tidings of her," answered Roger; "it is too likely that all on board have perished."

After much more information had been exchanged, Roger, with Vaughan Audley, returned on shore. Others would have done so, but the captain hoped to sail in the evening, and it was the object of all to reach James Town as soon as possible. Lettice was unwilling so soon again to part with Roger, but now, knowing that he was safe, her spirits revived, and the colour once more returned to her cheeks.

The wind proving favourable, the *Deliverance* and *Patience* got under way, and proceeded round to Cape Comfort, where they came to an anchor in the roads, not far from where the *Rainbow* and two other ships lay moored. Scarcely had their sails been furled than the wind, which had for some time been increasing, began to blow a perfect hurricane; the thunder roared, the lightning flashed, and the rain came down in torrents. Truly, they had reason to be thankful that they were in a safe harbour instead of being out on the stormy ocean. So fiercely did the hurricane rage that no boats could venture to pass between the ships. It was hoped that Vaughan and Roger had already safely reached the ship, but even of that they were uncertain. Hour after hour the storm raged on; the surface of the harbour was broken into foaming waves, which rolled hissing by. The tall trees on shore bent before the blast; huge boughs were seen torn off and whirled far away through the air.

All night long the hurricane continued. Towards morning it broke. When daylight returned, the clouds disappearing, the sun shone forth, brightly sparkling on the tiny wavelets, which now danced merrily on the bosom of the harbour. Early in the morning Gilbert, accompanied by Fenton, pulled on board the *Rainbow*. As he stepped on deck, Captain Layton, who was standing near the gangway, started on seeing him; for a minute or more it seemed that he could not believe his senses.

"Who are you, young man?" he exclaimed, scanning his features. Gilbert briefly told him who he was, and what had occurred.

"Heaven be praised!" exclaimed the captain; "I fully believed that you and all on board the *Sea Venture* had perished, or I should long ere this have gone in search of you. The news that your brother has escaped will restore life to my daughter Cicely, who has been mourning him as lost. I will at once go below and break the intelligence to her, or it may reach her too suddenly. Can I tell her that your brother is well?"

"I believe so," answered Gilbert. "He but yesterday landed with your son, and I expected to have found them on board the *Rainbow*. Why they have not arrived I cannot tell, as they were to have set off immediately from Fort Algernon."

"Possibly they may have been detained by the storm, but I would rather they had been here," observed the captain. "The state of the whole country is unsatisfactory, for the natives are often hostile, and it is dangerous for a small party to move far from the settlement, although it was understood that the Indians in this neighbourhood were friendly. However, we will not anticipate evil, but hope for the best."

While the captain was below, Gilbert and Fenton talked over the non-appearance of Vaughan and Roger, and agreed, should they not soon arrive, to set off in search of them with as many men as they could obtain. After some time the captain summoned them into the cabin. Cecily had been weeping tears of joy; she was anxious to make inquiries about Mistress Audley and Lettice. After they had replied to her many questions, the captain proposed visiting the *Deliverance*. Lettice and Cicely were delighted to meet each other, but their happiness would have been greater had Vaughan and Roger been present. They had already begun to feel anxious at their not having arrived on board. Captain Layton tried to conceal

from them his own apprehensions, but he expressed
them to the admiral and governor, who, at his request, agreed to furnish him with a party of men to
go in search of them should they not soon appear.
Gilbert, Fenton, and Oliver Dane obtained permission to join the expedition.

The party amounted to nearly a score, and with
their firearms, provided they acted with due caution,
had no need to fear any number of hostile Indians.
Captain Layton's intention was to proceed to the
fort, and should Roger and Vaughan have left it,
follow their trail with the aid of a friendly Indian
who was, he said, living there with the white men.

The country was in most parts open, but at times
they had to proceed by a narrow path cut through
the dense forest, where hostile natives might have
attacked them to great advantage, as they could
not have been seen till close upon them, and thus
their firearms would avail them but little. Oliver
Dane kept near the captain, who remained at the
head of the main body, while Gilbert and Fenton
went on some little way ahead with Ben Tarbox
and another man, peering into the forest at every
step to discover whether it harboured a foe. They
had got within nearly a mile of the fort when
Gilbert, who was looking through some bushes on
the right, beyond which the forest opened out
somewhat, caught sight of a figure moving rapidly
in the direction of the fort. He signed to his companions to remain concealed while he more carefully
surveyed the stranger, whom he soon knew, by his

dress of skins and the feathers which adorned his head, to be an Indian. Gilbert watched, supposing that others would follow, but the Indian was apparently alone. He was doubting whether he should advance or allow the Indian to proceed on his way, when the keen eye of the latter caught sight of his face amid the foliage. Gilbert now observed that, instead of a bow and quiver of arrows, he carried a musket in his hand. He knew, therefore, that he must have intercourse with the English, and was probably a friend. Signing to his companions to remain quiet, he advanced beyond the shelter of the bushes, and made a sign that he wished to speak with him. The stranger, showing no signs of fear, immediately came forward and inquired who he was and whither he was bound. Gilbert at once replied, that he and his companions were searching for two Englishmen who had come from the fort and were on their way to the ships in the roads.

"Then we are engaged on the same errand," said the Indian. "Know me as Miantomah, a friend of the pale-faces. I was in the fort when the ships arrived, and a young stranger came on shore. He and another officer immediately set off to the harbour. They had gone some few hours when one of my people, who had been out scouting, brought word that the Monacans, who are at enmity with the pale-faces, were out on a war-path, and would too probably fall in with the trail of our friends and pursue and scalp them. I at once offered to follow and warn them of their danger, and to lead them by a path round by the shore which the Monacans were not likely to approach. I hoped to have come upon them at their encampment, but they travelled more rapidly than I had expected; and while still on their track, night overtook me. Next day, at dawn, I pushed forward; but when I reached the spot where I calculated they must have encamped, to my dismay, I came upon the trail of the Monacans, who must, knew, have espied them. I went on, however, desirous of learning what had happened. I soon afterwards came upon the Monacan camp, and beyond it I found the trail of the two pale-faces. Could they by rapid travelling still have kept ahead? I feared not.

"Going on, I reached their camp; and now I learnt what had befallen them. They were still asleep on the beds they had formed of leaves, with their camp fire at their feet, when the Monacans had pounced on them before they could rise to defend themselves. There were no signs even of a struggle,—no blood was spilt; thus I hoped that their lives had been spared. I immediately followed the trail of the Monacans and their captives, which turned away to the west. I had not gone far when a fearful storm began to rage, and I knew well that those I was following would seek for some place where they might obtain shelter from the rain, which came down in torrents, and from the boughs of the trees falling around, torn off by the wind. I, nevertheless, pushed on; but the rain and wind had obliterated their trail, and I could only guess the direction they had taken. Before me, at some distance, was a rocky region in which several caverns existed, where the Monacans, should they be acquainted with them, would, I knew, fly for shelter. It was now necessary for me to advance with the greatest caution, lest I should be discovered by my foes, from whom I guessed that I could be at no great distance. I was compelled, for the sake of concealing myself, to travel through the forest; but I kept to those parts where the trees were of less height and the branches smaller, thus not being so likely to be torn off by the wind. The Monacans had, as I expected they would, escaped from the forest, and continued through the

more open country, and I at length caught sight of
them as they were making towards one of the
caverns I have spoken of. I watched them till
they took shelter within it, and then, crouching
down under the trunk of a fallen tree which afforded
me some slight protection from the tempest, I remained till nightfall. I knew that they would
kindle a fire at the mouth of the cavern, the light
from which would guide me to it; I was not disappointed, and, creeping cautiously along under
shelter of the rocks, I got near enough to hear
their voices. Close to the mouth of the cavern
was another, with a small entrance, penetrating
deeply into the hill, and communicating with the
large cavern. I did not hesitate to enter, hoping
to have an opportunity of speaking to the two pale-
faces, and, perhaps, even of rescuing them. I
waited till I supposed that all the Monacans were
asleep; then, groping my way, reached the end of
the cavern, and found myself, as I expected, at the
inner end of the large one.

" The Monacans had, I suspected, placed their
prisoners at the inner end for greater security. The
cavern was in perfect darkness, for the light of the
fire at the entrance did not extend thus far, though
it enabled me to see the people sleeping round it.
The noise of the tempest, the crashing of rocks as
they rolled down the hillside, the huge boughs
torn off from the trees, and the ceaseless rattling of
the thunder, drowned all other sounds, and I had
no fear of being heard. Cautiously I crept forward,

with my head bent to the ground, till I found myself close to a man, as I knew by his loud breathing. I felt his dress, and I thus knew that he was one of the prisoners. I put my mouth to his ear and whispered till I awoke him. He was the young sea-captain whom I knew. I told him that I had come to set him at liberty. He replied that he could not go without his friend, whose foot was hurt so that he could not escape by flight. That mattered not, I replied, as I could conceal him till the Monacans had got tired of looking for him.

Without loss of time, I released my friend, and we quickly set his companion at liberty. Helping him along between us, we crawled up to the hole by which I had entered. The Monacans, not suspecting what was going on, slept soundly. We crawled through the hole into the further end of the small cavern; here I believed that we were safe, as the darkness would prevent the Monacans from discovering our trail; and not aware, as I concluded, of the existence of the hole, they would be unable to guess by what means their prisoners had escaped."

Miantomah had got thus far in his narrative when Captain Layton and the rest of the party came up, and the Indian had to repeat what he had said, which, as he spoke in broken English, took some time. Gilbert, meantime, was very impatient to hear what farther had happened to his brother and Roger.

"And when you got into the end of the cavern,

what did you do?" he asked at last. "Are they there still?"

"I found that the young stranger, though unable to walk, could limp along with the assistance of his friend and me," continued Miantomah; "I knew of another cavern a short distance off, higher up the hill; if we could reach it, while the rain continued to pour down as it was still doing, we should be safe. I persuaded him to make the attempt. By remaining where we were we should too probably be caught, like burrowing animals in a hole, as the Monacans were not likely to go away without thoroughly searching both the caverns. The young man resting on our arms, we set out; the influence of the tempest, as before, prevented the sound of our footsteps reaching our enemies. At length we reached the mouth of the cavern, the position of which I well knew. Thick bushes grew in front of it, so that no strangers were likely to find us, but in case any of the enemy might pass by, I led my companions higher up the hill and then down close to the rock inside of the shrubs. Here we might be secure, though our enemies would not fail to search for us. There was but one way to draw them off the scent; I undertook to adopt it. I would get to a distance and let them see me, when they would to a certainty follow in my trail. Being fleet of foot, I knew that I could keep ahead of them. I waited till nearly daylight, when I knew they would discover the escape of their prisoners.

"Then descending the hill, I took my post at a distance from the cavern, where I could be seen by the Monacans as they issued forth. I was soon seen as I knew by their gestures, and uttering a loud shout and waving my gun over my head, I darted off. Being fast of foot, I knew that they could not overtake me ; and they probably thought that my object was to lead them into an ambush of the palefaces, for in a short time their cries no longer resounded through the forest, and I felt confident that they had turned back. I was even now on my way to the fort to obtain assistance, but if you will accompany me much time will be saved and we may the sooner reach your friends."

The meaning of this address being fully understood, Captain Layton at once agreed to Miantomah's proposal. Notwithstanding the long run he had had, he did not beg for a moment's rest, but led the way at a speed which taxed the strength of all the party. Gilbert especially was anxious to go to the rescue of his brother and Roger, for notwithstanding the assurances of the Indian, he could not help fearing that they were in the most perilous position. Should the Monacans discover them, they would in all probability instantly put them to death.

"They know what they are about," observed Fenton, "and depend upon it they will not allow themselves to be taken."

"Had they their arms they might defend themselves," observed Gilbert, "but of those the Indians are sure to have deprived them."

They asked Miantomah : he laughed. "I forgot to say that I secured both their weapons as well as their powder-flasks, and should their ammunition last, they would be able, from the mouth of the cavern, to keep at bay any number of assailants."

The party pushed on, stopping but a brief time to refresh themselves, till at the close of the day their guide told them that in a couple of hours more they might arrive at the caverns. Their leader's intention was accordingly to set off before daybreak, so as to reach the neighbourhood of the caverns soon after dawn, when the Indians, if still there, would be taking their morning meal. There was still much cause for anxiety, for should they suspect the trick that had been played them, and cunning as they were they were very likely to do so, they would certainly search every place in the neighbourhood in which the escaped captives were likely to have taken refuge ; for they well knew that Vaughan Audley was unable to walk, and that his companions could not have carried him far on their backs. A strict watch was kept by Captain Layton during the night, lest the natives might discover them and attempt an attack. The night however passed over quietly, and at the hour proposed, Miantomah, rousing up the party, led the way towards the hills. The birds were saluting the early dawn with their tuneful notes, when, just as the hills came in sight amid the trees, a shot was heard, followed by another.

"On! on!" cried the Indian guide. "Our friends have been discovered, as I feared, and are defending themselves; but, though they may hold out for some time, their ammunition must soon be expended, when the Monacans will, to a certainty, not spare their lives."

These remarks were not required to hasten the steps of the party. Gilbert, incited by love for his brother, dashed on at the top of his speed, followed by Fenton, Oliver Dane, and Ben Tarbox; even the Indian could scarcely keep up with them. The sound of shots continued to reach their ears; it encouraged them, showing that their friends were still holding out. In a short time they could hear even the shouts and cries of the Indians, as they climbed the hill, endeavouring to reach the mouth of the cavern; but, as yet, their approach had not been discovered. Miantomah now signed to them to keep to the left, and to crouch down as he was doing, following one after the other so that they might get close to their enemies before they were seen. His advice was followed, and the whole party were within gunshot before the Monacans were aware of their approach. For some seconds no shots were heard from the cavern, towards the mouth of which the Indians were seen shooting clouds of arrows, and then making their way up the hill as if they no longer expected resistance. On this, Miantomah, raising a loud war-whoop,

signed to the English to fire. He was obeyed : as
the smoke cleared off, several Indians were seen
stretched on the ground, while the rest went rushing
down the hill. Gilbert and several others were
about to follow them, when Captain Layton shouted
—"Keep together, my men, and reload, for the
savages are more numerous than we are ; and should
they get among us with their tomahawks our fire-
arms will be of no avail."

It was fortunate that this order was given, for
the natives, incited on by one who appeared to be
their chief, quickly rallied, and observing the small
number opposed to them, drew their bows and sent
a flight of arrows among them, which slightly
wounded two men. They were then about to dash
forward to meet the pale faces, uttering loud war-
whoops, and flourishing their tomahawks, when
Captain Layton ordered his men to fire and quickly
to reload, directing several to aim at the chief. A
loud shout reached their ears ; the Indians were
still rushing on, when his tomahawk was seen to
fall from their leader's hand, and the next instant,
while still in advance of his men, he came heavily
to the ground. His followers were still advancing,
when another volley was fired into their midst,
which brought several down and put the rest
hastily to flight, at a rate which would have rendered pursuit fruitless. Miantomah was about to
rush on, Indian-like, to take the scalp of the fallen
chief, when Captain Layton shouted to him to desist,

and dashed forward in time to stop his uplifted knife.

"Let us show mercy to our enemies," he exclaimed, as he stooped over the chief, who, resting on his arm, looked defiantly at those who surrounded him. In the mean time Gilbert, who was looking towards the cavern, caught sight of Roger Layton, who trampling aside the bushes, appeared at the entrance. Roger beckoned to him eagerly, and with several others he hurried up the hill.

"You have arrived opportunely," he exclaimed, "for Vaughan is sorely wounded, and I am but in little better plight."

Gilbert, making his way through the bushes, saw

his brother lying at the mouth of the cavern with
his musket by his side, the blood flowing from a
wound caused by an arrow in his side, but which
he had with much courage extracted, while Roger
showed the places in his dress where two others
had passed, one through his arm and another in
his leg ; a large number also sticking in the ground
around them.   Gilbert, with the assistance of Ben
Tarbox, quickly bound up his brother's wound,
Fenton and Oliver attending to Roger.   More men
being summoned to their assistance, their two
wounded friends were borne down the hill.

Captain Layton had attended to the wounds of
the Indian chief, which his experience told him
were not likely to prove mortal.   He deemed it
important, however, to get at once surgical assistance ; and as Roger informed him that that could
not be obtained at the fort, he determined, though
the distance was greater, to return forthwith to the
ships.   Litters were accordingly formed for the
conveyance of the wounded men, and the party
immediately set off, under the guidance of the
friendly Indian.   As they advanced, a vigilant
watch was kept in case the defeated Indians
should venture to follow and attempt the recovery
of their chief.   No natives, however, were seen ;
yet it was possible that they might be near at
hand, keeping themselves carefully concealed.

" This country may be a very fine one, and supply a fellow with as much tobacco as he can want

to smoke," observed Ben Tarbox; "but to my mind it isn't the pleasantest to travel in, when a man doesn't know when he goes to sleep whether he will get up again, not to say without his night-cap, but without the scalp on the top of his head."

From the judicious precautions taken by their leader, the party escaped attack, and arrived safely at the harbour. Vaughan and Roger were carried on board the *Rainbow*, which afforded more accom-modation than the other ships, and here, by Captain Layton's invitation, Mistress Audley and Lettice removed, that they might assist Cicely in taking care of the wounded men. The captured chief was also carried on board the *Rainbow*, for want of room in the other ships. He was here carefully tended by the surgeon and by Mistress Audley, Lettice and Cicely also paid him frequent visits; he thus quickly recovered, and seemed grateful for the care bestowed on him. His name, he said, was Canochet, chief of the Monacans; he had formed a wrong opinion of the pale-faces, believing that they were cruel tyrants, instead of kind and humane people, as he had found them. To Mistress Audley especially he seemed greatly attached, and he de-clared that he would willingly give up his life for sake of doing her a service.

Miantomah having performed his duty, returned to Fort Algernon, promising ere long to visit his new friends at James Town. The arrival of Mis-

tress Audley induced Captain Layton to change his
intention of returning to England, and the *Rainbow*,
accompanied by the *Perseverance* and *Patience*, proceeded up to James Town, situated about fifty
miles from the mouth of the river.

The settlers had expected to see a well laid-out
town, with broad streets and good-sized houses,
instead of which rows of huts alone were visible,
with here and there a cottage of somewhat larger
size; the whole surrounded by stockades. It was
situated on the borders of the river, which here
made a sharp angle, another stream running in on
one side. Thus the land on which it stood was
almost an island, and consequently protected from
any sudden attack by foes not possessed of boats or
canoes.

The owner of one of the larger cottages was
willing to dispose of it to Mistress Audley; and
Captain Layton having concluded the arrangement
for her, she and her family took up their abode
there. It faced the river, with a garden reaching
to the water in front. On each side there was a
broad verandah, affording shelter from the hot rays
of the sun. Mistress Audley, as might be expected,
invited Cicely to reside at the cottage, while Captain Layton and Roger were engaged in building a
house near at hand; they, in the mean time, living
on board the ship. The unfriendly disposition of
the natives compelled the settlers thus to concen-
trate themselves in a town, instead of forming

farms scattered over the country some distance from each other, by which means corn and other productions might, in that fertile region, have quickly been obtained. As it was, they had to depend on the chase, and on such provisions as they could purchase from the natives, who, though at first willing enough to part with food in exchange for the articles brought by the English, had of late brought in but a scanty supply. The state of the settlement also was in other respects unsatisfactory; the chief persons in authority had quarrelled with each other, and Captain Smith, the only man who had exhibited wisdom and energy, had lately started on an exploring expedition up the country, in the hopes of forming friendly relations with the chiefs and some of the more powerful tribes to the northward. It was hoped, however, that Sir Thomas Gates, aided by the energetic admiral, would bring things into better order.

The spirits of those who left England with bright hopes of soon becoming possessors of magnificent estates in the New World were thus at a low ebb, and had they not either embarked all their property in the enterprise or come out because they possessed none in England, the greater number of the settlers would ere this have returned. Vaughan and Roger had completely recovered from their hurts, and even the chief Canochet, though so severely wounded, was almost well again. He had been offered his liberty, but he replied that after having been so mercifully treated by the English he would not leave them till he had learned more of their language and religion. In this he was especially intructed by good Master Hunt, the chaplain, who had ever proved himself a friend to the Indians, and to his own countrymen, whose unseemly disputes he had been instrumental in settling.

Vaughan and Gilbert, having seen their mother established in her new home, were eager to set out in search of their father. She, however, knowing the dangers to which they would be exposed, was very unwilling to let them go until they had become somewhat acquainted with the language of the natives and the nature of the country. The two seamen, Tarbox and Flowers declared their belief that the spot where they had taken Batten on board was less than fifty miles to the north of the entrance to James River, and that consequently the place where he had met Captain Audley could not be much farther off than that distance from James Town. Captain Layton, however, who examined the men, was somewhat doubtful of the accuracy of their statements; still, although the distance might really be very much greater, he hoped in time by means of friendly Indians to hear if a white man was living with any of the tribes in that direction. At present no one in the settlement possessed a sufficient knowledge of the interior of the country to lead a party, especially among savages who would probably prove hostile. Roger and Gilbert wished to set out by themselves, but Captain Layton positively forbade his son going, and Mistress Audley, by his advice, put the same prohibition on Gilbert. They had therefore to restrain their impatience; Mistress Audley praying that God in His good providence would in time point out the way by which their object might be attained.

CHAPTER VI.

OME time had elapsed since Canochet had left his new friends, promising that the war-hatchet should be for ever buried betwen his tribe and the English. The settlers had begun to grow corn and tobacco, as well as to form gardens in which vegetables of all descriptions were produced. The surrounding natives visited them occasionally, but exhibited much want of confidence, which it was the object of the governor to overcome. He issued strict orders that all the Indians appearing among them should be treated with courtesy and kindness, and any chiefs coming to James Town were invariably sent away with presents and assurances of the good-will of the colonists. Still it was a hard matter to do away with the ill-feeling which existed in consequence of the hostile meetings which had previously occurred between the colonists and the Indians, in which many on both sides had been slain. At this juncture, one evening, as the settlers were returning to their dwellings, the labours of the day being over, the sentry posted on the look-out tower at one of the corners of the stockade, gave notice that an Indian in hot haste was approaching the town. As he came near he was recognized as an Indian named Pomaunkee, who had frequently been at the settlement, and who appeared to have a friendly feeling for the whites, although many disputes had occurred between them and his people, in which several of the latter had been killed.

He brought, he said, disastrous intelligence. Captain Smith and his followers had been attacked by a large body of Indians, who had murdered all but the captain, who having been overcome after a desperate struggle, had been carried captive to Powhattan, their chief. He also, probably, Pomaunkee declared, would be put to death, unless Powhattan would agree to receive a ransom for him.

The news, which was generally believed, created much dismay and excitement among the colonists. Pomaunkee was conducted to the governor, who examined him by means of an interpreter to satisfy himself of the truth of his report. The Indian, however, persisted in his statement, and at length the governor was convinced of its correctness. Those attached to Captain Smith expressed a desire to send out a party to rescue him, and all were ready to pay any ransom demanded. Among his warmest friends was Master Rolfe, Lettice Audley's old admirer. He had been prevented by an attack of illness from accompanying him, and was now most eager to set off; Vaughan, Gilbert, and Roger begged that they also might go. It was an opportunity not to be lost. Neither Captain Layton

nor Mistress Audley could withhold their consent.
As they were getting ready, Fenton and Oliver Dane
came and offered their services; they were aware of
the risk, but they could endure fatigue as well as
older men, and such danger as was to be encountered
they did not dread. Gilbert was very glad to find
that they were to go. As the two seamen, Tarbox
and Flowers, were supposed to have some acquaintance with the natives, they were also selected to form
part of the expedition which was placed under
Master Rolfe's command. Pomaunkee offered to
act as guide; and though the governor somewhat
doubted his fidelity, his services were accepted.

The party, thoroughly armed and confident in
their numbers, set off in high spirits, glad to have
escaped at length from the daily routine of the settlement. Mistress Audley, Lettice, and Cicely could
not see them depart without feeling much anxiety.
Captain Layton would gladly have accompanied
them, but a long tramp on shore did not suit his
legs, he observed; and he had moreover to look
after the ship and to be ready to protect Cicely and
Mistress Audley and Lettice. The expedition had
been kept as secret as possible, that the natives
might not hear of it and give information to the
neighbouring tribes.

Roger, Fenton, and Oliver had been up for some
time, eager to set off, and at early dawn the whole
party filed out of the town, taking a course to
the north-west. They proceeded rapidly, as it
was important to escape the observation of any

of the natives visiting the town who might carry information of their approach to Powhattan. As far as they could discover, they were observed by no one, and several miles were accomplished without a native being met with. The country through which they passed was in some parts open and level, in others covered by dense forests, many of the trees being totally strange to them. They had to cross numerous limpid streams, so that they were in no want of water. Several deer started from their coverts in the forest and bounded away over the plain, sorely tempting the travellers to follow them; but Master Rolfe, like a wise leader, forbade his men to separate in chase, lest the natives might take occasion to attack them. Gilbert and Fenton generally marched together and brought up the rear; it was the post of danger, but they were both known to be active and intelligent, and would keep as bright a look-out as any of the party. As they marched on, they held converse together.

"What think you of our guide, Pomaunkee?" asked Gilbert; " I watched him when we halted for dinner, and it struck me that I had seldom seen a less attractive countenance, or one more expressive of cunning. I expressed my opinion to my brother Vaughan, but he replied that Master Rolfe has perfect confidence in the man, having had frequent intercourse with him."

" I agree with you," answered Fenton. " I too watched him when he did not observe me; and it will be well to keep a look-out on him, though we must take care not to let him discover that he is suspected."

Evening was now approaching, when Rolfe, who had a soldier's eye, was looking out for a fit place for encamping. At a little distance he espied a rocky knoll rising out of the plain, with a stream flowing round its base on all sides. He at once saw that it would be a good spot for camping and might serve at some future time for the establishment of a fort. Pomaunkee, however, to whom he pointed it out, urged that they should continue on a mile or two farther, observing that the forest would afford greater shelter and warmth during the night, and that he would conduct then to a more fitting spot on the bank of a river.

" I am very sure that your proposal, Rolfe, is the best," observed Gilbert, who overheard the Indian's remark ; " we shall be the better for a cooler air at night, and moreover free from mosquitos on the top of the knoll. Allow Fenton and me to explore it, and we will quickly bring you word whether it is likely to prove as suitable for encamping as you suppose."

Rolfe having consented to this, Gilbert and Fenton set off. They quickly came to the conclusion that a better place for camping at night in an enemy's country could not be found, as, with proper vigilance, they were not likely to be surprised ; and, if attacked, could easily defend themselves against vastly superior numbers, especially if they had time to erect stockades at the more assailable points. The river, which flowed round three sides, was too deep to be forded; while rough rocks, a dozen or more feet in perpendicular height, formed the greater portion of the remaining side. They hurried back with this information, and, encountering Vaughan, who had come to meet them, persuaded him to induce Rolfe to act as he proposed, in opposition to the Indian's suggestions. Pomaunkee could scarcely conceal his annoyance; he, however, being unable to offer any further reason for proceeding, was compelled to follow the commander. Preparations for camping were soon made: some brushwood at the foot of the knoll was cut down to supply fuel. Gilbert, whose suspicions of Pomaunkee were increased by the opposition he had offered to the selection of the place, suggested that some stout stakes should be cut, and fixed on the side of the hill where the slope, being less abrupt than in other places, might be more easily mounted.

While these arrangements were being made, Gilbert and Fenton, who had been, according to their intention, watching Pomaunkee, saw him descend the hill and go in the direction of the forest. In a short time they lost sight of him among the trees.

"We ought not to have allowed him to go," observed Gilbert; "and even now I would advise Rolfe to send some men after him to bring him back, in case he may purpose to desert us altogether."

"The sooner we do so, then, the better," said Fenton; and together they went to Rolfe, who was at the time on the other side of the hill, and told him what they had observed.

"The Indian, I know, is faithful," he answered; "and I cannot suppose that he has any intention of playing us false."

Vaughan, however, agreed with Gilbert, and at length persuaded Rolfe to send Tarbox and

Flowers, with two other men, to follow the Indian and to bring him back, should it appear that he was deserting them. Meantime, the fires were lighted, pots were put on to boil, huts formed with boughs were set up to serve as a shelter from

the night air, and all other arrangements for the
night encampment were made. It was nearly dark
when Tarbox and the other men with him returned,
stating that they had once caught sight of Pomaunkee in the distance, but before they could get
up to him he had disappeared, and that after having
searched in vain, they had judged it time to return.

"His disappearance without telling me of his
intention, looks suspicious," observed Rolfe, "and
I thank you, Gilbert and Fenton, for the warning
you gave me. He may intend treachery, or he may
simply have grown weary of guiding us, and, Indian
fashion, have gone off without thinking it necessary
to tell us of his intention. In either case, we will
strengthen the camp as far as time will allow."

"For my part, I am glad to be rid of him,"
observed Gilbert; "and, aided by our compass, we
can find our way without his guidance."

Supper was over; the watch was set, the officers
were seated round their camp-fire, discussing how
they should proceed on reaching Powhattan's village on the morrow, when the sentry gave notice
that an Indian was approaching from the side of
the forest.

"After all, we have wronged Pomaunkee, and he
is returning," observed Rolfe.

"Not so certain of that," remarked Vaughan, who
had now begun to entertain the same opinion of the
Indian as his brother; "he may have been absent
on an errand not tending to our advantage, and it
will be well, if we do not hold him in durance, that

we watch him even more narrowly than before."

" Let us, at all events, learn what he has to say for himself," observed Gilbert, rising. Vaughan and Fenton accompanied him. The Indian ascended the hill, and the sentry, believing him to be their guide, allowed him to pass without challenge. As he got within the ruddy glare of the fire, instead of the forbidding countenance of Pomaunkee, the far more pleasant features of the Monacan chief, Canochet, were brought into view. Vaughan and Gilbert greeted him warmly.

" I am thankful that I have arrived in time to warn you of intended treachery," said the chief. " He who undertook to be your guide, has formed a plot for your destruction. I gained a knowledge of his intentions, and instantly followed on your trail to warn you. On passing through the forest, I found that you had come hither, and was following you when I caught sight of the traitor. I tracked him, unseen, till I found he had joined a large body of his tribe, who are lying in ambush about a mile from this. On discovering them, I had no doubt that he intended to betray you into their hands. As I thought that even now he might hope to attack you unawares, I hastened to bring you warning, that you might be prepared, should he attempt to surprise you. I myself would remain, but my single arm could not avail you much, and I should render you more aid by returning to my people, who, though they are still at a distance, I may yet bring up in time to assist you."

Rolfe, on hearing this, thanking Canochet for the warning he had given, begged him to hasten on his tribe, though he doubted not that he could hold out against any number of savages Pomaunkee might collect to attack him.

"You call them savages," observed Canochet; "but remember, except that they do not possess firearms, they are as brave and warlike as you are; and as they know the country and are full of cunning, they are not to be despised. Take my advice: do not be tempted to quit your present position till I return with my people. Depend on it, it will be their endeavour to draw you away, so that they may attack you when you are encamping in the forest or open ground."

"Your advice seems good, my friend," answered Rolfe; "but suppose you are delayed? We shall starve here, unless we can procure food."

"Trust to my return before that time arrives," answered Canochet; "I will endeavor to supply your wants. I must no longer delay, as every moment is precious. It is my belief that you will be attacked this night, so be on the watch. However hard pressed by numbers, do not yield."

"You may depend on our holding out to the last," answered Rolfe; and the Indian, without further remark, descended the hill, making his way down among the rocks, so that, had any one been watching at a distance, he could not have been

I

discovered. Almost before he had reached the bottom of the hill he had disappeared, and even Gilbert's keen eyes could not detect him as he rapidly penetrated into the forest.

"If Canochet has spoken the truth, we have had a narrow escape," observed Vaughan. "We shall do well to take his advice and to remain here, whether we are attacked or not, till his return."

To the wisdom of this, Rolfe and Roger Layton agreed, eager as they were to hasten to the rescue of Captain Smith. Having completed their fortifications as far as their materials would permit, six of their party were told off to keep watch, while the rest lay down to sleep.

Roger took command of the first watch, for he suspected that the Indians would attack them during the early part of the night. On going round to the sentries, he found them standing upright, their figures clearly discernible against the sky to any one approaching on the plain below. Pointing out to them the danger to which they thus exposed themselves, he directed them to crouch down, so that an enemy might have no mark at which to aim.

"I fear, sir, that some of our fellows may be apt to fall asleep," observed Ben Tarbox, who was one of those in the first watch.

"Do not trouble yourselves about that," answered Roger; "I will take good care that they keep awake. If any one of you catch sight of a moving object, do not fire till you hail, and then, if you get no answer, take good aim, and do not throw a shot away."

The men promised obedience. There was little chance, while Roger Layton was on watch, of the fort being surprised. The first watch went by without the slightest sound being heard, or an object seen outside the camp. The second was drawing to a close, when Ben Tarbox exclaimed: "Who goes there? Stand up like a man, or I'll fire at you!" His shout caused all the sleepers to raise their heads. The shot which followed made them seize their weapons and start to their feet! Scarcely had the sound of the shot died away, when the most terrific cries and shrieks rent the night air, followed by a flight of arrows which whistled over the heads of the garrison as they hurried to the stockades, and a hundred dark forms showed themselves endeavouring to make their way amid the rocks up the hill.

"Let each of you take good aim," cried Roger, "and load and fire as fast as you can."

The order was obeyed; the officers, who had also firearms, setting the example. The Indians, who had expected to surprise the white-faces, found themselves exposed to a blaze of fire from the whole side of the hill, up which they were attempting to climb. Still, urged on by their leaders, they mounted higher and higher, in spite of the many who fell, till they reached the stockades. Some of the more daring, attempting to hack at the English with their tomahawks, were pierced with pikes and swords wielded by the stout arms of Rolfe, Roger Layton, the Audleys, and Fenton; while their men kept firing away as rapidly as they could reload their weapons. The Indians fought bravely, but unprepared for so determined a resistance, they at length gave way, and retreated, one driving back the other down the hill. Some were hurled over the rocks by the victorious garrison, who, led by Roger, sprang out beyond the stockades, and in another minute not a living Indian remained on the hill.

"Hurrah, lads! we've beaten them!" shouted Ben Tarbox, giving a hearty hurrah, such as he would have raised on seeing the flag of an enemy come down in a battle at sea.

"Let no one go beyond the stockades," cried Rolfe, "we know not what trick they may play us; let us not lose the advantage we have gained."

He spoke in good time, for Roger and Gilbert were on the point of rushing down the hill in pursuit of the flying enemy. The wild uproar which had lately reigned suddenly ceased; not a sound was heard—even if any of the wounded Indians lived, they did not give vent to their sufferings by uttering a single groan; and, as far as the garrison could discover, the whole body of their foes had retreated to a distance. The young leaders of the English, aware of the cunning of the Indians, were not to be deceived; every man continued at his post, watching all sides of the hill beneath them on which the attack had been made, as well as the

others round which the river flowed. Gilbert and
Fenton had gone to a rock overhanging the stream,
a few bushes growing amid the crevices of which
afforded them shelter. Thence they could look
down into the dark water almost directly below
them. Their muskets rested on the rock, so as to
command the passage; the only sound heard was
the occasional cry of some night-bird, which came
from the neighbouring forest. Harry Rolfe, Vaughan, and Roger continued moving round the hill,
to be sure that the sentries were keeping a vigilant
watch. They knew that the enemy they had to
deal with was not to be despised. Although there
was no moon, the stars shone down from a cloud-
less sky, casting a faint light over the plain. Two
hours had gone by; the third was drawing on;
Gilbert and Fenton occasionally exchanged a few
words in a low whisper, to assist in keeping each
other awake. At length Gilbert was looking out
directly ahead of him, when he caught sight, amid
the tall grass, of an object slowly approaching. It
seemed at that distance like a huge serpent making
its way towards the river; now it stopped, and the
grass almost hid it from view; now it advanced,
getting nearer and nearer the river. Gilbert, afraid
to speak, touched Fenton's arm, and pointed it out
to him.

"Is it a panther?" asked Fenton.

"No," answered Gilbert; "that is the head of
a band of Indians; I can trace them following one
after the other. Wait till their leader reaches the

bank; I will aim at him, and you take the second. Their intention is to swim across and attack us unawares; if they persevere, we will raise a shout which will quickly bring our comrades to oppose them."

Whether or not Gilbert's voice reached the keen ears of the Indians it was difficult to say. The dark line remained perfectly quiet, and he almost fancied that he must have been mistaken. At length, however, it again moved on, and he could distinguish the form of an Indian crawling along the ground, followed closely by another advancing in the same manner. The first reached the bank, when, without even raising himself, he glided down it, and, sinking noiselessly into the water, began to swim across. The next followed in the same manner.

"Now," whispered Gilbert; and aiming at the swimmer, he fired. Fenton did the same. A cry rang through the night air: it was the death-shriek of the second Indian. The first disappeared, and Gilbert concluded that he had sunk, shot through the head, beneath the surface. Rolfe, with Vaughan and Roger, came hurrying to the spot, followed by several other men. Gilbert, pointing to the opposite bank, exclaimed, "There they are!" A volley was fired. Whether or not any of the Indians were hit, it was impossible to say; probably, finding themselves discovered, they had dispersed on all sides, and crouching down beneath the grass, fled to a distance.

"We have foiled them again!" exclaimed Gilbert, exultingly; "they will not venture another night attack, I've a notion."

"We must not trust to that," observed Rolfe; "they are as persevering as they are cunning, and, though defeated half a dozen times, they may hope to succeed on the seventh. That was but a small party who have just now retreated, and it may be that the main body are watching their opportunity to attack us on the other side."

"I believe that you are right," said Vaughan; "we must make up our minds to keep on the watch till daylight, for even now the enemy may be lurking round us, though we cannot see them."

Vaughan, while speaking, was standing up on the higher part of the knoll, whence he could view the plain on every side.

"If there should be any Indians near, you are affording them a good mark, brother," exclaimed Gilbert. Just as he spoke an arrow whistled through the air close to Vaughan's head and flew completely over the knoll. It was evidently shot by a person at the base, close down to the river.

"I thought that I had killed the Indian," exclaimed Gilbert, "but he must have found his way to the shore. If we are quick about it, we shall take him prisoner—who will follow me?"

"I will! and I will!" cried Fenton and Tarbox, leaping down the hill.

"Stay, stay," exclaimed Rolfe, "there may be others lurking near."

Gilbert and his companions did not hear him,

and in an instant had reached the bank of the river at the spot from whence they supposed the Indian had shot his arrow. They searched around, however, on every side, but could find no one. Rolfe, still fearing for their safety, again more peremptorily summoned them back. They returned much disappointed at not having made the capture they expected. It was scarcely possible, they thought, that the Indian could have crossed the river, and if so, he must still be lurking concealed beneath a rock or bush on the side of the hill, and might at any moment appear among them, and strike a blow in revenge for those whom they had killed. To escape this fate, Rolfe ordered the men to stand with their swords drawn and their eyes on every side. Thus a single Indian had the power of keeping the whole camp awake and wearing out their strength.

It still wanted nearly an hour to dawn, and before that time they might be engaged in a more desperate conflict than the first. They could only hope that Canochet would soon arrive to their relief. They would not fear to encounter ten times as many as themselves in the open ground during the day, but it would be madness to attempt to march through the country when they would be certain to be attacked at night by overwhelming numbers. With grateful hearts they welcomed the appearance of the dawn, which as it rapidly increased exposed to their view the surrounding country and the hill-side, on which lay the bodies of four Indians, who had been

shot dead during the attack. On the opposite side
of the river they discovered the body of the native
shot by Fenton; none of the bodies, however, as far
as could be judged from their costume, appeared to
be those of chiefs.

As soon as it was broad daylight, Rolfe allowed
Gilbert and those who had accompanied him at
night to continue their search for the Indian who
had shot his arrow at Vaughan. He could nowhere,
however, be found, and they concluded therefore
that he must have floated down the river, and landed
at some distance from the hill. Not wishing to allow
the dead bodies of the Indians to remain near them,
they were dragged to the bank and allowed to float
down with the current.

As their provisions were running short, they
anxiously looked out for the arrival of Canochet,
who, they hoped, would ere this have come to their
assistance. Something, they concluded, therefore,
had detained him. The fire was now lighted, and
they cooked their morning meal.

" Should the chief not soon appear, I propose
that we set out without waiting for him," said
Roger; " not finding us at the fort, he will
follow in our trail, and after the lessons we have
given the Indians, they are not likely again to
attack us."

Rolfe and Vaughan, however, thought it would be
more prudent to remain where they were.

" Provided we had food, I should agree with you,"
answered Roger, " but starvation is a tough foe to

fight against, and for my part I would rather face a whole host of Indians."

Still, as Canochet might certainly be expected in the course of the day, Rolfe was not moved from his purpose. The party did not fail to keep a bright look-out from their hill; chafing, however, at the delay to which they were subjected. Gilbert and Fenton especially, with most of the men, were eager to go on. Their last piece of venison was consumed, and they were growing very hungry. As the two young men were seated together on the top of a rock whence they could look out round them on every side, Fenton exclaimed, " See, see, Gilbert! yonder is a deer—she just showed her head from behind that thicket on the borders of the forest—there is some sweet grass there probably on which she is browsing. If we could steal up from to leeward, we might get close enough to shoot her before she discovers us."

Gilbert looked in the direction Fenton pointed, and he too seeing the deer, agreed that the opportunity of obtaining a supply of venison was not to be lost. Slipping down from the rock, they made their way round the base of the hill till they reached a spot directly to leeward of the thicket near which they had seen the deer browsing. From thence they advanced cautiously amid the high rocks and bushes till they got close to the forest, believing every instant that they should see the animal before them.

" She must have gone round to the other side,"

observed Fenton; and they crawled on further. On looking back, Roger observed that they were almost out of sight of the hill. Still, eager to get the deer, they went further on, when they again caught sight of the head and shoulders of the animal, grazing not where they expected, but a considerable distance off in the forest. They might hit the creature, but should they miss, it would certainly be lost to them; they therefore determined to get nearer. At last, Gilbert was rising to his feet to fire, when he heard Fenton utter a cry; bitterly had they cause to regret their folly in having quitted the shelter of the fort.

CHAPTER VII.

TARBOX and Flowers had been on the watch on the side of the hill looking towards that part of the forest where the seeming deer had appeared, and had observed the young officers making their way in that direction. Remembering the proverb, that "too many cooks spoil the broth," they were afraid that were they to go also, the deer would escape, and they might lose their share of the venison. They waited, therefore, with much eagerness, for the return of the sportsmen. When, however, time went by and they did not appear, Tarbox, calling to Roger Layton, told him what had happened.

" Can you nowhere see them ? " asked Roger.

" No, sir ; maybe the deer has led them a long chase," answered Tarbox.

" The Indians may be lurking about," observed Roger to Vaughan, who just then joined him. Vaughan naturally felt anxious, and at once proposed taking half a dozen men and going in search of the two lads. Roger insisted on accompanying him. Rolfe charged them to be cautious, for, knowing the guile of the Indians, he feared greatly that Gilbert and Fenton had fallen into their hands, and that they themselves also would run a great risk of being surprised.

"We will keep our eyes about us," said Roger, springing down the hill to the side of Vaughan, who, with six volunteers, had already reached the bottom. They hurried on, keeping their firearms ready for immediate use; for, though they still hoped that Gilbert and Fenton had really gone in chase of a deer, they knew that at any moment they might fall in with the Indians. On reaching the forest they advanced more cautiously than at first, every now and then stopping and shouting out to Gilbert and Fenton; but no reply coming, they pushed on still further.

"The lads would scarcely have been so foolish as to have chased the deer further than this," said Roger. "I very much fear that the Indians have caught them."

"I fear the same," answered Vaughan, with a sigh, as if unwilling to acknowledge the truth; "but if so, would they not have slain them at once rather than have carried them off prisoners?"

"We will, at all events, make a further search through the forest," said Roger. "We must not give up all hopes of finding them."

Though aware that they were acting imprudently, they could not resist the temptation of going on farther, the whole party looking out among the trees; but nothing could they discover to enlighten them on the subject. They were about to turn back, when Ben Tarbox, who was a little way off on the extreme right of the line, shouted that he saw a deer feeding at some distance ahead, and, holding his gun ready to fire, he ran on in the direction he pointed. Presently the report of his gun was heard, and the rest of the party hurrying up, saw the deer, which, strange to say, had not moved. On reaching it, great was their surprise to find only the head of the animal supported by a stick in the ground, with the skin of the back fastened to it.

"Why, this is the very deer we caught sight of," exclaimed Tarbox; "it shows pretty clearly the sort of trick the Indians have played the young gentlemen, and tells too truly what has happened to them; though why their decoy was left behind is more than I can say."

Vaughan and Roger knew that Ben was right; the only question now was, whether they should try to overtake the Indians and endeavour to rescue their friends, if still alive, from their hands. Vaughan soon came to the conclusion that they could not hope to do so, and, with a sad heart, acknowledged that they must at once return to the camp.

"We shall have to fight our way to it, then," exclaimed Roger; "see there!"—and he pointed in the direction from whence they had come, where, amid the trees, appeared a large body of savages. As soon as the Indians found that they were dis-covered, they set up a fearful war-whoop, their cries and shouts echoing through the forest; while, drawing their bows, they shot a flight of arrows, by which, happily, no one was wounded.

"Reserve your fire," exclaimed Roger, "till we get near enough to make sure of our men: their shouting and shrieking will do us no harm."

Again the savages uttered a war-whoop, and seemed about to rush forward to attack the small party of whites with their tomahawks, when their shouts were replied to from the opposite part of the forest.

"Was that an echo, or are those the voices of another party of Indians?" exclaimed Vaughan; "if so, between the two we shall have a hard fight of it to make our way back to the camp."

Another war-whoop sounded from behind them, and looking in the direction from whence it came, they could distinguish a still larger party than that in front coming quickly towards them.

"Keep together, lads, and we'll cut our way through those between us and the camp," exclaimed Roger; "and if the others follow, we must turn round and keep them at bay till we can get the assistance of our friends."

Drawing their swords, Roger and Vaughan led the way towards their foes. Greatly to their surprise, the Indians, instead of stopping to receive their charge, turned round and fled away through the forest to the westward; while, from the opposite side, the other party was seen advancing rapidly. Roger and Vaughan, determining either

to defeat them or to sell their lives dearly, ordered
their men to be ready to fire when they should give
the word. As they were about to do so, they saw
a tall Indian whom, even at that distance, they
knew by his dress to be a chief, advance some way
ahead of the rest, holding up in his hand a branch
which he waved to and fro.

"Stay," exclaimed Roger, rushing before the
men. "Do not fire—they are friends."

As the Indian advanced they recognized Canochet,
whom they now hurried forward to greet. In a few
words they explained what had occurred, and entreated him to give chase to their late opponents,
whom they could not doubt had carried off Gilbert
and Fenton. On looking round, however, they found
that the whole band, whom they had just before seen
at the end of the forest, had disappeared. Canochet
immediately waving to his men, ordered them to advance in pursuit of the foe, and no sooner had he
uttered the word of command than a hundred
warriors, bow in hand, were rushing through the
forest at a rate with which the party of English
found it a hard matter to keep up. Every instant
they expected to come in sight of their flying foe,
but on reaching the border of the forest, not an
Indian was to be seen. Canochet, with some of
his men, sagacious braves, searched in vain for the
trail of the enemy; it was evident that they had
turned off either to one side or the other, and that
they had missed it, while eagerly pushing forward
in pursuit. He was of opinion that they had made

for the stream, and having followed it up where the shallow water allowed them to wade, they had crossed to the opposite side and made their way to the northward.

The question whether they had got hold of Gilbert and Fenton still remained unsettled, till Canochet heard of the discovery of the deer's head, when he had no longer any doubt about the matter.

" The youths were deceived by the seeming deer, and have been entrapped by their foes—an Indian would have been too wise to be caught by so simple a trick," remarked the Monacan chief.

" They were indeed foolish," observed Vaughan, with a sigh ; " but have their captors put them to death, think you ? "

Canochet considered an instant : " Revenge is sweet," he observed ; " but an Indian can be moved by other motives. They may have deemed it prudent to preserve their lives, either to exhibit them to their tribe as trophies of victory, or to exchange them for any of their own people who may be captured— though I must not conceal from you that the women and relatives of those who have been slain will certainly demand their death. It is believed, however, that our great chief Powhattan, from having preserved the life of Captain Smith, is favourable to the English; and they may dread his vengeance more than that of the whites, should they injure their young captives."

This information afforded but doubtful comfort to Vaughan and Roger; they would be ready, they said, to pay any amount of ransom for their friends, if Canochet could manage to communicate with their captors. He promised to do so, and at once sent off a party to discover their trail and to follow them up; though he acknowledged that he had no great hopes that they would be overtaken. In the mean time, he and the rest of his band, accompanied by Vaughan and Roger, proceeded to the camp. They had now still more reason than ever to hasten their visit to Powhattan, in the hopes that he might assist in the recovery of the captives should their lives have been spared.

Rolfe ordered his men to get into marching order, and, accompanied by the Monacan chief, they proceeded on their journey. The day was already far spent, so that they had gone but a short distance before it was necessary to camp, in order that the hunters might go out in search of game. There was no slight danger to the huntsmen, for Pomaunkee's people might possibly have followed them, and be on the watch to cut off any one leaving the camp. Hunger, however, overcame their fears, and the huntsmen returned in safety with three deer, sufficient to afford food both to the English and natives. The fires had already been lighted, and the cooks at once set to work to roast the joints of venison, on spits formed of wood, supported on forked sticks; while the rest of the Indians squatted round with eager eyes, watching the process.

The Indians, confiding in their numbers, seemed to consider that no attack would be made on them, but Rolfe, after the experience he had gained of the treachery of the natives, deemed it prudent to place sentries round his part of the camp. He advised Canochet to do the same. " We are not so careless as you suppose," answered the chief; " we have men on the watch, but we deem it unwise to allow them to stand up so that they may afford a mark to the enemy. We conceal our watchmen from the foe approaching the camp, so that he never knows when he may be discovered; we have men on guard out-side your sentries, so that if it pleases you, they may lie down and rest."

After hearing this, Rolfe and the other leaders slept far more soundly than they otherwise would have done. The night passed away without in-terruption, and the next morning they proceeded on their way. Vaughan anxiously inquired of Ca-nochet when he expected the return of his people. He had directed them, he said, merely to follow the trail to ascertain the direction the enemy had taken, and to gain as much other information as they could pick up. It was not, however, till late the next day that the party overtook the main body of the Monacans. They had discovered a trail which led towards the north, and that two white men were with the party, they were from the first certain. That this was the case was confirmed by a slip of paper which had been found fastened to a tree by a thorn. It contained but a few words, signed by Gilbert; Vaughan eagerly took it. " We are both alive, but our captors glance at us unpleasantly.

We will try to escape; follow if you can, and help us."

Vaughan explained the meaning of the words to Canochet. " Wonderful ! " he exclaimed ; " can so small a piece of white material with a few faint strokes on it say so much ? "

He promised to follow the Indians, as Gilbert had desired; Vaughan wished to set out at once with him, but he recommended that he should first communicate with Powhattan, and get his assistance. Vaughan, though still very anxious, was somewhat relieved, and agreed to follow the chief's advice.

Towards the evening, as they were proceeding along the banks of a broad stream which fell in a succession of cascades over its rocky bed, Canochet informed them that they were approaching the abode of the great chief. He had sent on before, as in duty bound, to announce their coming. Rolfe and Vaughan, accompanied by Canochet, were marching ahead of their party, the English following them, and the Indians at a little distance behind; they had just turned an angle of the river, beneath the shade of some lofty trees which stretched their branches far over the water, when they saw standing before them a man of tall stature and dignified mien, clothed in rich skins handsomely ornamented, a plate of gold hanging on his breast, and an ornament of the same precious metal on his head. By his side was a young girl who could scarcely, from her appearance, have seen seventeen summers. The

pure blood which coursed through her veins and
mantled on her cheeks gave a peculiarly rich hue to
her skin, while her features were of exquisite form ;
her eyes large, and of a lustrous blackness. On her
head she wore a circlet of feathers ; her raven locks,
parted at her brow, hung down in long plaits behind
her slender waist. Altogether, Rolfe thought he
had never seen so beautiful a creature. Though
Vaughan could not fail to admire her, the blue eyes
and fair face of Mistress Cicely were more to his
taste. Fortunately for Rolfe, he had no difficult
diplomatic duty to perform, or he might perchance
have been tempted to yield too easily, won by the
bewitching graces of the lovely savage.

The chief received the strangers with dignity as
they advanced towards him. He had heard of their
coming, he said, and gave them welcome. His wish
was to be on friendly terms with them, and the people
of their nation, one of whom, a great chief he seemed
and full of wisdom, was even now his guest. Rolfe,
who already spoke the native tongue with considerable fluency, replied, in suitable language, that he
was grateful to the chief for the words he had let
fall ; that his guest was indeed a man of renown—
his more than father and friend—and that it was
with the object of visiting him, as well as to pay his
respects to the mighty Powhattan, that he and his
followers had made the journey into his country.
The English had come, he added, with no hostile intentions : the land was large enough for the natives

and themselves; and their desire was to live on friendly terms with all around them. He invited Powhattan to come to the town they had built and to judge for himself.

The Indian seemed well pleased with this address. "And now," he said, " come with me to my home ; such entertainment as I can give is prepared, and my wish is that when you go hence you may say that Powhattan has treated you in princelike fashion."

Rolfe now made further inquiries about Captain Smith. The chief replied that he was in safe keeping, though he acknowledged that he had not hitherto thought fit to allow him to go abroad.

" In other words, he keeps him a strict prisoner," observed Vaughan; " we must insist on his being forthwith set at liberty, or he may think fit to detain him when we wish to take our departure."

" I will not fail to follow your advice," answered Rolfe, who then turning to the chief, remarked that his heart yearned to see his honoured friend, and that he begged he might without delay be brought into his presence.

" My daughter, Pocahontas, shall conduct you," said the chief, after some consideration. As they proceeded on, he spoke a few words to his daughter. " He is in her charge," he remarked, "for as she preserved his life, she demanded that he should be placed under her protection."

" I could not desire a better guide," answered Rolfe, bowing to the chief's daughter. They had now arrived before a village composed of houses of a more substantial character than those of the Indian villages hitherto seen. While the chief proceeded towards the largest, in the centre of the village, Pocahontas, taking Rolfe's hand in obedience to her father's command, led him towards a hut on one side, before which, hatchet in hand, was a sentry. Meantime Canochet drew up his warriors on the open space in front of the chief's house, while Vaughan ordered his men to halt also near the same spot, in the neighbourhood of which a number of women were congregating with baskets full of provisions.

Each moment that Rolfe was in the company of the Indian maiden, he was more and more struck by her beauty, her graceful carriage, and modest manners and intelligence.

" You are the second paleface only I have seen," she observed, artlessly; " your brave chief was the first. I saw the gallant way in which, when attacked by my countrymen, he defended himself, seizing one of our most noted warriors and holding him before himself as a shield; till slipping on the moist soil he fell, with numbers surrounding him. Before he could recover himself he was overwhelmed and bound, and led captive to my father. I felt horror at the thought that so brave a man should be put to death, and such as would have been his fate had I not at the moment our braves were about to strike, thrown myself before him and prayed my father to spare his life."

" Bless you, lady, for the merciful act," exclaimed

Rolfe, gazing at the young girl with greater admiration even than before, " my friend must bless you too, and my countrymen, when they hear what you have done, will endeavour to show their gratitude."

" They can best show it by remaining at peace with my people," answered the maiden, looking up in his face, though, as her eyes met his glance of admiration, she turned them again to the ground. She opened the door of the hut; Captain Smith, who was seated on a mat on the floor, started up, and on seeing Rolfe, sprang forward to meet him.

" I was sure that, should you hear of my captivity, you would not rest till you had made every possible effort to rescue me," said the captain ; " were it not for this fair lady, your efforts would, however, have been useless."   He took the hand of Pocahontas and raised it to his lips.   She smiled at the act of courtesy, so unlike any to which she had been accustomed.

" She has already told me that she was the means of saving your life," observed Rolfe, " and I have been endeavouring to tell her how grateful I and all those who esteem you feel to her.   She has now come to set you at liberty, and the chief will raise no objection to your returning with us.   Whether he gives us leave or not, we have determined to carry you off. I will try to induce him to accompany us; it will be of much importance to get him to visit James Town, where he can see our houses, and ships, and great guns, and other things wondrous to him.

It will give him a proper notion of our power, and the means we possess of defeating our enemies should they attack us."

Rolfe, as they walked through the village, explained to Pocahontas their purpose, and by his descriptions of the wonders possessed by the English he raised an ardent desire in her mind to go and see them. The banquet provided by Powhattan need not be described : it was somewhat of a barbarous kind, though the viands were not to be despised. Contrary to the Indian custom, Pocahontas was present, seated on a mat near her father, with Rolfe next her; while Captain Smith and Vaughan sat on the other side. Vaughan being unable himself to converse with the chief, got Rolfe to tell him of the loss of their two companions, and to beg that he would use his power to recover them.

" They must be far away by this time to the northeast, and though those who have captured them own my sovereignty, they are wont at times to act independently of me. However, I will take steps to recover your friends." Such was the substance of the answer given by Powhattan. Vaughan then reminding Rolfe of his main object in coming to the country, begged him to inquire of the chief whether he knew of any Englishman held captive for many years by his nation. Powhattan replied that rumours had reached him of palefaces having been seen in different parts of the country, but that none of them having been brought before him, he could not at present give his guests any exact information on the subject; but he would on that point also, he promised, make inquiries. He seemed pleased at the confidence they showed him, when they expressed their readiness to occupy a part of his dwelling, separated from their men. After the fatigues they had gone through, they slept soundly.

CHAPTER VIII.

LTHOUGH the object of their expedition had been gained, Vaughan's heart felt sad as he thought of returning to James Town without his brother. Powhattan had expressed his intention of accompanying the party, with his daughter, to visit the English governor; no longer, therefore, were difficulties or dangers to be apprehended, as no foes would dare to attack the powerful chief; while his hunters would bring in an ample supply of game. Had Gilbert and Fenton not been missing, he would still have felt that his great object—the discovery of his father— seemed no nearer than before; for neither from Powhattan nor Canochet had he been able to obtain any information about him. Canochet gave him hopes that Gilbert and Fenton were still alive, and would be recovered; but till the appearance of the party sent in pursuit of their supposed captors nothing certain could be known.

The chief having made up his mind to visit the English, was eager to set off; he was attended by fifty of his braves, dressed in their gayest costume; he marching, however, on foot, while his daughter was conveyed in a litter, cushioned with skins, and canopied with boughs to shield her from the hot rays of the sun. Very different was her lot from that of the other women of the tribe, who were, the Englishmen observed with no little disgust, compelled to labour hard from morning till night, while their lords and masters lolled in the shade and smoked their pipes.

While Captain Smith marched in front with the chief, Harry Rolfe often found himself by the side of Pocahontas, with whom in her own language he managed to converse. He told her of the wonders of the ocean, of the mode by which the ships found their way across it, of England, of its great cities, its magnificent palaces, its superb temples, its armies of horse and foot, with their guns, dealing death and destruction among their foes, and capable of battering down strong walls. The Indian maiden listened with wondering ears ; for some time she spoke not, at length she sighed. Rolfe inquired what grieved her.

" That I can never hope to see the wonders you speak of. Till now, I thought my father the most powerful king on earth, and you have shown me that our people are but children compared to those existing beyond the mighty ocean."

To the latter remark Rolfe made no reply, as he did not wish further to wound the maiden's vanity. " Would you desire to visit those distant lands and see the wonders I have been describing ? " he asked.

"I cannot leave my father and my people," she answered. "But go on—tell me more about your country—I will try to bring the scenes you describe so well before my eyes."

Rolfe continued, as desired; and the Indian girl seemed never weary of listening to him. Thus, whatever others might have done, he found the journey too speedily brought to an end. The governor received the Indian chief in a becoming manner, with all the pomp he could assume. Banners were flying, music playing, and guns firing. The sound of the artillery especially seemed to affect the chief; and when he saw a shot fired across the river strike a tree and tear off a large branch, he lifted up his hands in wonder, and exclaimed, "Who can stand against a people so armed?"

Vaughan had hastened home with a sad heart to break the intelligence of Gilbert's loss to his mother. At her house he found Captain Layton, who had already heard through the forethought of Roger what had occurred.

"Do not be cast down, Mistress Audley," he said, after Vaughan had given her the account; "we have certain notice from Gilbert himself that the Indians did not kill him and Fenton when they were first seized; and the savages well know that it will be more to their interest to preserve their lives than to take them; and as they tell me that the great chief who has just come to the settlement has no small power among the people of this country, we may trust to his being able to recover them before long. I have much hope, also, that with his assistance we may at length find your husband. I had determined, on the return of my son, to sail along the shore of the Chesapeake, and to make inquiries among all the natives I can meet with. Should Powhattan not be able to help us as we hoped, I shall forthwith carry out my plan. My two seamen have now come back; I will question them afresh. And now that they have seen more of the country, they may be able to say whether it was here or elsewhere they met with the poor wretch Batten : would that he had lived—he would have helped us more than they have done, or are likely to do."

While Mistress Audley's spirits were somewhat revived by Captain Layton's assurances, she received a message from the governor, requesting her to act the hostess to the Indian princess just arrived with her father. This she could not refuse ; and Lettice and Cicely were well pleased with the thoughts of having the Indian maiden under their care. Accordingly word was sent to the governor that they were willing to receive her as their guest. In a short time Pocahontas arrived, still seated on her litter, with Harry Rolfe by her side. Mistress Audley, with Lettice and Cicely, went forth to meet her, and taking her hand as the bearers placed the litter on the ground, helped her to rise, and led her into the house, followed by Harry Rolfe, who seemed unwilling to give up the charge of the damsel even to them. The beautiful young savage, for such, in the presence of the English matron and the two young maidens, she truly seemed, cast looks of admiration at their fair features, and their dresses, which appeared to her of wondrous texture. Although they could exchange but a few words with her, they were able with the assistance of Harry Rolfe to answer her questions; and in a short time she appeared perfectly at home with them.

At length she asked whether they were Harry's sisters, and hearing that they were not so was silent, looking up first to one, and then to the other, and then towards Harry himself; and it could be easily seen that her brain was busy though her tongue was silent. A hut had been prepared for the chief, suitable to his wants, though bearing little resemblance to a royal palace. He came the next day to see his daughter, and appeared to be so well pleased with the treatment she received, that he intimated to the governor his intention of leaving her for a while with her new friends. His proposal was gladly accepted, as it proved his good feelings towards the English, and the confidence he placed in them. Captain Layton and Vaughan, with the assistance of Harry Rolfe, had a long talk with him. Regarding Captain Audley he promised to make inquiries among the tribes of his nation. While they were speaking, the head of the party sent out to follow the trail of the Indians who had carried off Gilbert and Fenton arrived. He and his people had traced them, he said, far to the

north, when they found themselves in the country
of a hostile tribe, from among whom they had
great difficulty in escaping. On hearing this, Powhattan was exceedingly wroth, and threatened to
punish the Annaboles, the tribe spoken of, who owed
him, he affirmed, allegiance. Rolfe, however, en·
treated that he would employ mild measures, lest
the Annaboles might retaliate on their two prisoners.
This information was on the whole unsatisfactory.
Gilbert and Fenton might, it was hoped, be still
alive, but that they had been carried to a distance
was certain, and their recovery would be difficult,
as Powhattan, notwithstanding his boasted power,
could, it was clear, afford them no assistance.

"It seems to me, Vaughan, that we must trust
to our own strong arms and mother-wit to recover
the two lads," observed Captain Layton, when they
had parted from the chief. "What say you,
Roger?"

"I hold to your opinion, father; if we could get
together some thirty trusty fellows, and the means
of carrying our provisions, we would march from
one end of the country to the other, and compel
those knavish Indians at the point of our swords to
deliver up their prisoners," answered Roger; "we
might then, perchance, fall in also with Captain
Audley, if he is, as I trust, still in the land of the
living."

"Those 'ifs' and 'ans' are stubborn things,"
observed the captain.

"We might, however, manage to carry provisions

on our shoulders for a week or more," said Roger, "and thus be enabled to march for three or four days inland from the shore, and back again without the need of hunting, provided we could keep in the open country, and not get entangled among forests or rocky defiles where our foes might pick us off without our being able to reach them."

"I know not whether we should gain much by that, unless we could manage to surprise an Indian village, and capture some of their chief men to hold as hostages till they agreed to give up their captives. These Indians are very different to the cowardly tribes we have been wont to meet with on the Spanish Main, as experience should already have taught you," observed the captain : "still, with discipline and determination we shall be able, I doubt not, to tackle them. I like your proposal, however, and as soon as we can get a crew together, we will sail up the Chesapeake and try what we can do."

Vaughan, grieved by the long, though unavoidable, delay which had already occurred, was willing to take part in any plan his friends proposed, and they accordingly at once set to work to collect a crew for the expedition. They had, however, except the promise of good pay, no inducements to offer. Had they proposed an expedition to the Spanish Main they would speedily have collected as many men as they required ; but as only hard knocks were to be expected, without the chance of prize-money, those who would have had no objection to the two combined, hung back. The captain at length, in despair, promised that if men would come forward, and they should succeed in their enterprise, he would take a cruise in search of Spaniards, and that the prizes taken should be divided equally among all hands. This offer was likely enough to have succeeded, when a party who had been out hunting returned full of excitement, with the news that they had discovered a vein of gold, or as some said a mine, at a stream some six miles distant from James Town. The news spread like wildfire through the settlement, and every one was eager to be off with spades and pickaxes to gather up the golden treasure. The seamen who had engaged to serve on board the *Rainbow* were among the first to be off; those who were labouring in the fields left their ploughs; the few who had opened shops closed their doors and set out, for there were no buyers of their wares.

The governor and admiral, and a few other officers, remained at their posts. Captain Layton, in very vexation of spirit, refused to go even to look at the mines, declaring that "all is not gold that glitters"; and it might be, after all, this seeming gold was no better than dross; or that if gold it was, it would stay there till he had time to go and fetch it. Roger and Vaughan were of his opinion; indeed, neither would have left those they were bound to protect, were it to prove as rich as the mines of Peru and Mexico. Some days had passed

away, when some of the explorers came dropping
in, their backs heavily laden with sacks full, as they
said, of gold-dust.

"Mixed with not a little dross, I guess," observed Captain
Layton, who met
Ben   Tarbox
s t a g g e r i n g
along under as
heavy a load as
he had ever at-
tempted to carry
in his life. "Let
us see, let us
see thy precious
gold-dust," he
exclaimed. Ben,
letting the sack
drop   on   the
ground,   pro-
duced a hand-
ful.   The even-

ing sun was shining brightly, and the dust un-
doubtedly glittered.

"I have seen stuff like that before," observed
Roger, who just then came up, "and what do you
think it was worth, lads?—not the pains of moving
from where it lay."

"They say it be gold," exclaimed Ben, looking
somewhat aghast; "gold glitters, and so does
this."

"There the resemblance ends, my lad," observed Captain Layton. "If no better gold is to be got out of the mine up there than thy sack contains, the settlers have lost many a day's work, and the colony is so much the poorer; though, from all accounts, it is not seldom they have thrown away their time before."

"Then what can I do with this sackful of stuff?" exclaimed Ben, who, having unbounded confidence in his captain, fully believed what he said.

"Sell it to the first fool who will buy it of thee for what he thinks it is worth," answered the captain, laughing. "Make thy bargain when the sun shines, though, or he may chance to set a low value on it."

Ben, it was supposed, followed his captain's advice, for the next day at noon he appeared on board the *Rainbow* without his sack, but chinking some Spanish pesos in his pocket.

Captain Layton, as did the governor, the admiral, and Master Hunt, the chaplain, warned those who returned of the utter worthlessness of the stuff they had brought, but they were not believed; and the idea got abroad that their object was to appropriate it, and thus to gain the benefit of their labours. Most of them, therefore, as soon as they had deposited their treasure in such places of security as they could find, set off for a fresh supply; while the boldest speculator proposed to charter two or three of the remaining ships, and send them home loaded with the precious dust.

The first addressed himself to Captain Layton, offering him a cargo for the *Rainbow*.

"There are two reasons against accepting your proposal, good sir," answered the captain; "the first is that I have other occupation for my ship, and the second is that I have no wish to become the laughing-stock of people at home, should I arrive with a shipload of dust not worth carting on shore."

Thereat Master Jarvis turned away, highly indignant, remarking, "Fools know not their own interest." The captain smiled, but replied not, recollecting that to answer an angry man is but adding oil to the fire. Master Jarvis was more successful with the captains of two other ships, which, as fast as the toiling settlers could bring in their sacks of dust, took them on board, the vessels being filled up with sassafras and other woods, and a few small packages of tobacco, all deemed, however, but of little value compared to the glittering dirt, as Captain Layton called it. There was no lack of volunteers to man the ships, as all were promised shares in the proceeds of the cargoes. Not till they had sailed could Captain Layton obtain a crew for the *Rainbow*. He summoned the remaining mariners in the settlement, who, already grown weary of tobacco-planting and digging, and their backs aching with the sacks of dust they had brought from the mine, were ready for any fresh adventure proposed to them.

"Lads," he said, "there are two things I have

set myself to do : first, to look for the honourable
gentleman who has been held captive for many
years by the Indians ; as also for his son and young
Master Fenton ; and when we have found them, to
go in search of two or more Spanish ships, which
will put more gold into the pockets of each one of
us than will all the dust you have just sent home."

It might be that the remarks of the governor
and admiral, and more especially those of Captain
Smith, had by this time begun to open the eyes of
the settlers as to the real value of the said dust.
One thing was certain, that had they devoted their
labours to the production of corn instead of to the
digging and carrying of the glittering soil, they
would not have been so hard-pressed as they now
were.   Those who had come from the Bermudas
recollected the ample supply of provisions those
islands afforded.   The good admiral, Sir George
Summers, offered, though now sixty years of age,
to sail in the *Patience*, the stout pinnace he had
built, and to bring back a supply for the benefit of
the colony.   He asked but for a score of men to
accompany him; a few faithful hearts obeyed his
call, and with the hopes of finding their wants
speedily relieved, the colonists saw that true knight
sail away on his hazardous voyage.   Alas! they
were to see him no more ; overcome by the hard
toil he had so long endured for the good of others,
he had not long arrived when he yielded up his
brave spirit at those islands, which were, rightly,
for many years called after his name.

The appeal made by Captain Layton was not in vain. Ben Tarbox was the first volunteer, and others followed his lead. "And what, Señor Nicholas, are you not going to join us?" asked Ben of his old messmate Flowers, who winced, Ben observed, whenever thus addressed. "Art not to be tempted by the prospect of fighting the Dons, man, and pocketing some of their gold? Thou canst speak their lingo, for I have heard thee talk it in thy sleep."

"I have had enough of fighting in my time, and have come out here to end my days in peace." answered Flowers.

"Thou wouldst end them with a better conscience by repenting of thy misdeeds and doing a worthy act to prove thy sincerity," answered Ben. His arguments, however, could not move his former messmate, who refused to the last to accompany him. Vaughan was doubtful whether he ought to stay for the protection of his mother and sister and Cicely, seeing that Captain Layton was going away, or to accompany him in search of his father and brother; but the governor and Captain Smith promised to defend them whatever might happen, and even Mistress Audley urged him to go. Captain Layton could ill spare one good man and true, for with all his exertions he had been able to collect barely a sufficient number of followers for his object; and Vaughan, though brought up at college, had a strong arm and a stout heart, and he might, should the first part of the enterprise prove successful, return to the settlement without the necessity of sailing forth again to fight the Spaniards.

Thus the *Rainbow* sailed down the river, under the command of Captain Layton, with Roger and Vaughan as his lieutenants; and young Andrew Dane, who had begged hard to be allowed to go.

In the mean time, the Indian princess, as the settlers called her, was rapidly learning English and becoming accustomed to English ways and manners; but the period during which her father had promised to allow her to remain was drawing to a close, when he had said he would return to take her back to her home. Harry Rolfe was a frequent visitor at the house, as also was Captain Smith, who owing his life to her, could not fail to regard her with gratitude, if with no other feeling; but she was in age compared to him a mere child, and might have been his daughter. Still, when he came to the house, Mrs. Audley had some doubts as to the sentiments he entertained towards the Indian girl; nor could she discover how Pocahontas regarded him. Still, it did not become her to speak to him on the subject; but when the story became known of the way Pocahontas had saved the life of the brave captain, it was generally reported that he would certainly, should Powhattan permit it, make her his wife, and Harry Rolfe often heard the matter discussed. The governor was naturally well pleased at the thoughts of such an event taking place, as it would, he hoped, secure the friendship of Powhattan, and the active support of his tribe. Harry Rolfe had at first been struck by the unusual beauty of the Indian girl, and had become deeply enamoured. How matters would have gone had Lettice regarded him with that affection he once sought, it is hard to say ; but his cousin, though she received him in a friendly manner, treated him, it was evident, with indifference, and at length he was fain to acknowledge that his happiness depended on making the Indian girl his wife. Could he, however, hope to win her, should his commander, the bravest and wisest man in the settlement as all acknowledged, regard her with affection; if so, he might yield to him who had the prior claim, and he would go on board the first ship sailing, to make war on the Spaniards, or would engage in any desperate enterprise afoot.

It happened that day that Pocahontas, who, though an Indian princess, had the fancies and foibles of many of her sex, had taken it into her head that she would be dressed as her companions. Cicely's gown was too short and somewhat too wide; and Lettice, willing to please her, dressed her in the best she possessed; putting on her a hat with feathers in it. Scarcely had the three damsels appeared in the parlour, when who should arrive but Captain Smith, Mistress Audley coming in directly afterwards. He gazed with more astonishment than admiration at the young Indian, for the costume, though becoming enough to the fair complexion of Lettice, sat but ill on the Indian girl, accustomed to the free play of her limbs; its colour harmonizing worse with her dark skin. Forgetting the progress Pocahontas had made in English, he said with slight caution to Mistress Audley, in his blunt fashion, " You will spoil the little savage, Madam, if she is thus allowed to be made ridiculous by being habited in the dress of a civilized dame. I owe her a debt of gratitude for saving my life; but that does not blind me to her faults, and the sooner she is sent back to her father the better for her, I opine."

" My daughter simply wished to please her, and it is but a harmless freak," answered Mistress Audley, " though I acknowledge that her Indian costume becomes her best."

Pocahontas, who had understood something of what was said, casting an angry look at the captain, burst into tears—then, taking the hand of Lettice, she rushed out of the room.

" I had no intention of offending her," said Captain Smith, " but her manner proves that if she stays much longer here she will be spoilt."

" Heaven forbid ! " said Mistress Audley ; " our great wish is not only to instruct her in English manners, but to teach her the simple truths of the Gospel, that she may assist in imparting them to her benighted countrymen, and for that purpose I would fain keep her here as long as her father will allow her to stay. Master Hunt is assisting us in the work, which God's grace alone can accomplish, we being but weak instruments in His hands."

"That alters the case," observed the captain. "If you have any hope of success by all means keep her with you, but let her not indulge the fancy that a silk dress will enable her to become like an English maiden of high degree."

Mistress Audley promised to follow the captain's advice. Cicely put in a word in favour of their guest.

"Well," observed the captain, "I leave it with you, kind ladies, to make my peace with her"; and before Pocahontas returned he had taken his departure. Soon afterwards Harry Rolfe appeared; the agitation of her feelings had brought the colour into the face of the Indian girl, who he thought looked more lovely than ever, habited as she now was in her native costume. His eye showed this, if his words did not, and she understood him.

"You would not laugh at me," she said, in her artless way, "if I were to dress as your country-women; and such I wish to become"; and Rolfe told her honestly that in his eyes she would be lovely however habited. She showed her satisfaction in a way he could not mistake; he left the house convinced that her heart was his. Soon afterwards, meeting Captain Smith, he frankly told him of his love for the Indian maiden, adding, "But should you, my dear friend, entertain thoughts of her, I am resolved to quit the country and seek my fortune elsewhere."

"Stay and be happy with her," was the answer, "if wedding with one who is half a savage can make you so."

Whereat Master Rolfe, thanking the captain from
his heart, assured him that so rapid was the progress she had made that ere many weeks were over
she would be fit company for the proudest dames in
England, and much more of the same nature; at
which the captain smiled, and patting him on the
back, assured him that it mattered not, provided
Mistress Audley and her fair daughter, who were
the proudest dames in Virginia, were content to
treat her as their friend.

So Harry Rolfe went back and asked Pocahontas
in plain language to become his bride, to which she
willingly consented, telling him to let her settle the
matter with her father. Harry Rolfe looked forward with no little anxiety to the arrival of the
king, who came at length, attended by fifty warriors; at which the prudent governor, not knowing
how many might be behind, got all the men in the
settlement under arms, as if to do him honour, but
secretly keeping a strict watch on his movements.
He was convinced, however, that the king's intentions were honest, the more so when, after visiting
his daughter, he announced that she had his full
permission to marry the English chief, Harry
Rolfe. As Master Hunt, after consulting with the
governor, was willing to perform the ceremony,
the marriage took place before Powhattan quitted
James Town, much to the satisfaction of all the
colonists. The long harangue delivered by Powhattan need not be repeated, nor need the replies
of the governor, Captain Smith, and the happy

bridegroom. He, being no sluggard, had built a house for himself, to which he at once took his bride. Flags were hoisted, guns were fired, and the bell of the church (hung to the bough of a tree, as there was no steeple yet built) rang right merrily, and the people shouted till they were hoarse, believing that from henceforth war with the Indians was at an end, and that they might go on and prosper in the land.

CHAPTER IX.

THE *Rainbow* was some time making her way down the river, and we may be sure that Lettice and Cicely watched her till her white canvas was no longer to be seen amid the tall trees which lined its banks; and that Vaughan's eyes, at all events, as he stood on the poop, gazed back till their figures faded from sight. Roger was too much engaged in the navigation of the ship to take more now and again than a hurried look astern: he knew his duty too well to neglect it, even for that; for there were shoals to be avoided, and sails to be trimmed to catch the fickle wind.

Hampton Roads were not reached till dark, when the *Rainbow* had to bring up till the following morning. A bright look-out was kept during the night lest any Spaniard or other stranger might enter the harbour, and, finding a solitary ship, venture to attack her. At dawn, anchor was weighed, and the breeze being fair, Old Comfort Point was rounded, and the *Rainbow* steered northward up the broad Chesapeake. The lead was kept going, for Captain Layton desired to keep as close to the shore as prudence would permit; while Vaughan noted down each point and bay, and the mouth of every stream and inlet they passed.

"Dost know the look of this coast, Ben?" asked Roger, as he saw Tarbox gazing eagerly at the shore.

"Ay, marry do I, sir," answered the old sailor; "for we sailed up and down it for many a league in the *Sally Rose*, and I thought when I came to see it again I should not forget it."

"But you said the same when we sailed up James River," remarked Roger.

"And it is my belief that I once went up that also, with brave Sir Richard Grenville in his pinnace; but I was somewhat mazed about the matter, and when Nicholas Flowers, who had been with me in the *Sally Rose*, said he knew the place, I thought I must know it too; but now I come to see this coast, I find out that I was then wrong and am now right," answered Ben.

"You hav'n't got Nicholas by your elbow now to prompt you, so keep a sharp look-out, and be sure that you are right this time," said Roger.

"Ay, that I will, sir," answered Ben; "and every league we make good, the more sure I am that I am right."

"I believe that honest Ben is not mistaken, and that we may have a better hope of success than ever before," said Roger to Vaughan, when he joined him on the poop. The ship continued running on all day; but the wind was light, and her progress, consequently, slow. Towards evening she brought up in a deep bay, in which Ben declared the *Sally Rose* had come to an anchor on her downward passage. The next morning she continued her course, and had run on with a brisk breeze for some hours, when Ben shouted out— "That's the bay, sir, where Dick Sponson and I, when we had Batten with us, found the *Sally Rose*, after he had escaped from the Indians; it is three days' pull, in a heavy boat with the wind against us, to the northward of this, where we took Batten on board. I should know the place again almost as well as I know Dartmouth harbour. It was about six miles inland of that where our shipmates were killed. If we sail on at the rate we are now going, we shall reach it before noon to-morrow, always provided the wind don't head us."

This information was, at all events, satisfactory, and Ben was so positive that Roger could not but believe him. Ben added, that, to his belief, a short distance farther on there was a river, up which the long-boat might pull for many a league, and that he calculated it would take them into the very heart of the country where Batten, according to his account, had been. As they sailed on, Ben, every now and then, exclaimed—"I mind that point, for we were becalmed off it for the best part of a day."—"Yes, that hill is just where I thought to find one."—"We pulled up yonder stream to get a fresh store of water, and had to pull down it again pretty quickly, with only half our casks full, by reason of a party of Indians."

Thus he ran on, recognizing all the main features of the shore. The ship, however, did not reach the bay he had expected, and, accordingly, had to stand off the shore and bring up at night in a more open position than would have been chosen; but, as the weather was calm, that mattered not. Early the next morning, however, the bay he had indicated was reached, and some time before dark the ship came off the very spot where Batten had been taken on board. He knew it by the easy landing the shore afforded, and by two tall trees which leant over one towards the other as if affording mutual support. The spot for which Audley and Captain Layton and his son had been so eagerly looking was at length reached; as, however, it did not afford a secure anchorage, they determined to stand on in hopes of finding the mouth of the river into which they intended to run and bring up. It proved to be not more than a couple of leagues to the northward. Roger having gone ahead in the skiff to sound, piloted the ship to an anchorage just inside the mouth, where she could lie secure from any storms which might blow without, and at the same time too far from the shore to be assailed from thence by any hostile Indians; while her guns would enable her to defend herself against any attack which might be made in canoes, should the natives prove hostile. It being now nearly dark, nothing could be done on shore till the next morning. The night was perfectly calm; the stars glittering overhead were reflected on the mirror-like surface of the water. The forest extending down to the shores of the deep bay in which the ship lay formed a dark wall round her, from which, ever and anon, came strange sounds; but no human voices were heard to denote that the country was inhabited. Still, a strict watch was wisely kept, for the silence which reigned was no proof that the savages were at a distance.

Meantime, preparations were made for the proposed expedition; the captain would willingly have led it, but Roger persuaded him to remain on board and look after the ship. "Half a dozen men, with you to command them, will be of more avail than a score without you," he observed; "we may thus take twenty with us and leave enough in charge of the boat."

To this the captain at length assented, knowing well that he could not move as fast, nor endure as much fatigue as his younger companions. At dawn the boat shoved off, each man carrying provisions for a week's march, with a further supply in the boat, to be ready should they exhaust their stock before they could return to her. Twenty men, besides the two leaders and Oliver Dane, were to form the expedition. The rest were to remain in the boat. Quitting the river, Ben Tarbox piloted them to the very spot where he and his companion had recived Batten on board their boat.

"That is the direction from whence we saw him coming," he said, pointing to the north-west; "and by his account he had been making, as far as he

could judge, pretty straight for the shore, as he had
the sun, when it rose, directly in his eyes, and he thus
knew that he was holding on to the eastward."

"Then we will march in the direction from
whence he came," said Roger. "On, lads!" he
exclaimed, having given his last orders to the crew
to lie off the shore at anchor, and to allow no Indians on board under any pretext till his return.
The forest was tolerably open, and the boat's compass enabled them to keep the course they desired.
No wigwams were seen, nor cultivated fields, nor
did any natives make their appearance. Now and
then a deer started from before them : Roger and
Vaughan were too careful leaders to allow their men
to chase the animals, lest the natives might take the
opportunity of setting upon them while thus separated. "Better empty insides than cloven skulls, lads,"
observed Roger ; "ere long we shall have a deer
crossing our path near enough to bring it down
without the risk of being taken at a disadvantage."

The men, seeing the wisdom of this, marched
forward without complaint. Night coming on, they
camped in the centre of a tolerably wide space of
open ground, near which, at a little distance, ran a
stream from whence they could obtain a supply of
water, while the bushes which grew near it afforded
them fuel. Here also they might hope to get a shot
at some animal coming down to drink, which would
give them fresh meat and enable them to husband
their provisions. Vaughan had often carried a
fowling-piece amid the woods and hills of Devon-

M 2

shire, and was the best shot of the party; he accordingly volunteered to watch for a deer, keeping near enough to the camp to obtain assistance if required. It wanted but half an hour to sunset, at which time animals were most likely to come down to drink. Oliver, also carrying a gun, went with him. But few trees or shrubs grew on the banks of the stream, which ran foaming and bubbling over a stony bed, with rocks on either side. As the time was short, they had at once to select a convenient shelter: the best they could find was between a rock and a thick bush, which overhung the stream. Here, leaning against the bank, they could command the opposite shore, which shelved gradually to the water, as it did also some way lower down.

Vaughan was beginning to get weary of waiting, when he saw a couple of deer moving amid the tall grass and brushwood which covered the country for some distance on the opposite side : Oliver saw them also. Recollecting the way Gilbert and Fenton had been entrapped, he thought it possible that the Indians might be attempting to play them a similar trick. The deer trotted forward, and the wind coming from them, they did not discover their enemies, and reaching the bank, began to drink. Vaughan and Oliver raised their pieces, and as the deer lifted up their long necks, they fired together and both fell dead. A shout of triumph raised by Oliver brought several from the camp to the spot, who dashing across the river, the deer were soon cut up, and several pieces of venison were quickly roasting before the fire.

Their success encouraged them to hope that they might obtain ample food, and be able to prosecute their search much further than they had intended. The sound of the shot, however, and their fires, might attract the natives to their neighbourhood; and a very vigilant watch was therefore kept during the night. Somewhat to their surprise, however, it passed away quietly, and the next morning they resumed their march. They were passing the borders of a thick wood, nearly knee-deep in grass, when Roger felt his foot strike against a hard substance which emitted a hollow sound, as it gave way before him. Stooping down, he rose with a human skull in his hand, white and clean. He and Vaughan examined it: the top showed a deep cleft. Others at the same time cried out that they were walking among bones.

"Some Indian battle has taken place here," observed Roger.

"That is no Indian skull," said Vaughan, "but that of a round-headed Englishman. The blow which killed him, it is clear, was inflicted by an Indian tomahawk."

The men, who had been searching about, now brought up from among the grass several other skulls, each one giving the same indubitable evidence of the manner in which the owner had been slain.

"This must be the very place where Batten saw the crew of the *Sally Rose* slaughtered," observed Vaughan. "It proves that we are on the right track, and should warn us to be cautious in our advance, lest the natives play us the same trick."

Further search produced altogether ten skulls, the number, it was concluded, of the unfortunate party cut off. Their clothing and arms had evidently been carried away, the bodies alone being left as a feast for the vultures and armadillos. The incident was not encouraging; Roger, however, quickly revived the spirits of his party by remarking that all they had to do was to keep a watch on every side, and not to be cajoled by any tricks the Indians might attempt to play them.

Having already provisions for a couple of days, they pushed on bravely, and would have continued even longer than they had intended, had they not unexpectedly arrived on the banks of a broad river, to cross which without a boat would prove a difficult matter and a dangerous one, should Indians attempt to stop their landing on the opposite bank. They agreed therefore that their best course was to proceed up the river, and to borrow canoes, should they find them—as they had no doubt that it was the river at the mouth of which their ship lay, they could without difficulty return to her, provided they could find canoes of sufficient burden to carry them; and if not, they might descend the stream by a raft—no very hazardous undertaking to men such as they were.

It was high time to meet with Indians, and they hoped soon to do so, provided they could establish friendly relations with them, for by their means only could they obtain the information they required. They therefore marched on merrily, and having the river on their right, they had now only one side to guard. As the land was level and not thickly timbered, they could keep close to the water. As Batten had not spoken about a river, they concluded that he had not been carried to the north of the stream along which they were making their way, and that therefore they must be in the neighbourhood of the district in which he had been held captive. As they had cooked the remainder of their venison at their last halting-place, they judged it wise not to light a fire lest they might attract Indians to their camp at night, who might at all events disturb their rest. Thus Roger and Vaughan thought they might probably have passed Indian villages without being discovered. They came to two or three small streams, through which they waded, though the water was above their waists, while Ben Tarbox carried Oliver on his shoulders.

At length, however, another stream was reached too broad and deep to be crossed in this fashion; a ford might exist, they thought, further up, and they accordingly were proceeding along the bank when Roger's eye fell upon a canoe hauled up on the shore some way ahead. This would afford them the means of crossing, they hoped; but on reaching her it was found that she was formed of birch bark, that her side was battered in, and that she was indeed little better than a sieve. She was of no avail, therefore, for their purpose.

The existence of a canoe in that place went to show that the natives were not far off; still Roger and Vaughan determined to cross, as they were unwilling to get farther from the main stream. They set to work, therefore, to cut down a number of small trees to form a raft. While they were thus engaged, Vaughan with his usual companion, Oliver Dane, proceeded a little higher up along the bank in search of game, Roger cautioning them not to go far. In a short time Oliver came back, saying that he had caught sight of an Indian in a canoe, spearing fish amid some rapids which ran across the stream; but as the fisher had not seen him, they might easily go back without being discovered.

" If we can avoid alarming him, and get him to come to us, which he may do, by seeing only two persons, it may prove a favourable opportunity for obtaining information," observed Vaughan; "we must proceed cautiously, however, and I will keep out of sight while you make signs to the fisher."

They accordingly crept along behind some thick bushes which effectually concealed them from the person in the canoe. At length they reached the spot, whence Vaughan could see the fisher. "Why," he whispered to Oliver, "that is a young girl; but though her dress is that of an Indian, she appears to me at this distance fairer than even the Princess Pocahontas—a graceful young damsel, too. See, she has struck another fish, and is hauling it in. Do you, Oliver, go and show yourself on the bank; sing as you have been wont to do on board, and beckon to her; it will calm any alarm she might be inclined to feel, and she will come more readily than were she to see me."

Oliver did as he was bid. The girl just then caught sight of him, and as she did so, she laid down her lance and seizing a paddle, with a couple of strokes sent her canoe out of the rapids into the smoother water below them; then, lifting a bow with an arrow, drew it to the head. Just then Oliver, having found his voice, began to sing the first air which came into his head. The maiden stood balancing herself in her frail bark, motionless as a statue, listening with eager ears to the notes which reached her, then, slowly withdrawing her arrow, let it fall with her bow into the canoe. Oliver sang on, observing the effect of his music, and beckoned as he had been directed. She quickly understood him and sinking into her seat, with rapid strokes she urged the canoe towards the bank, her countenance turned with an eager and wondering gaze at his face. She came on till the bow of the canoe almost touched the shore; then, standing up, she beckoned him to come down to her from the top of the bank, when with another stroke of her paddle she brought the canoe close to him.

"Who are you? whence do you come?" she asked eagerly. Oliver knew enough of the Indian language to understand her, though scarcely enough to reply. He pointed therefore down the river, intimating that he came thus far in a big ship, though he said nothing of his companions. She appeared to comprehend him, looking up all the time eagerly as before in his face; then she put out her hand close to his as if comparing the colour; hers indeed was the lightest of the two. Next she pointed to her face, which though sunburnt, was not so dark as his. Her countenance showed the thoughts which were passing rapidly through her mind. At last she inquired his object in coming thither. He told her that it was to seek for some friends, white people, who were supposed to be in that part of the country. She stood with her finger on her brow for a minute or more, as if meditating what to do; then, having made up her mind, she took his hand and signed to him to step into the canoe and sit down. Oliver was a brave lad, and without hesitation he complied. No sooner was he on board than with one stroke of her paddle she sent the canoe away from the bank, directing its head up the stream towards the rapids down which she had descended. As she got near them she handed him another paddle, and intimated to him that he was to use it in ascending the rapids. He had frequently paddled about in James River in Indian canoes, and was therefore able to obey her. On seeing this, she uttered an expression of approbation. Vaughan, who had watched these proceedings with much interest, saw his young companion, and the Indian girl paddle on till they had reached smooth water above the rapids, when they darted away at a rate which quickly took them out of sight.

" He is a brave fellow to go thus unhesitatingly, and I trust that no harm will befall him; he probably was afraid of frightening the young damsel or he would have called to me, to ask my advice." Such was the tenour of his thoughts, as he made his way back to where he had left the rest of the party. Roger was highly pleased when he heard of Oliver's courage in going thus alone with the Indian girl, and agreed with Vaughan as to the motive which induced him to accompany her.

" One thing is certain," he observed, " that it will be useless for us to continue making the raft, as we must either wait Oliver's return here, or follow him up along the stream to the place to which the girl has conveyed him."

Vaughan agreeing that this was the best thing to do, the men were ordered to get into marching order.

After passing the spot near the rapids where the Indian girl had taken Oliver into her canoe, the ground
became very rough, a high and rugged ridge making
their progress, laden as they were, exceedingly difficult.   Still, they felt bound to follow Oliver, for the
maiden's friends might not be disposed to treat the
lad as kindly as she might, supposing him to be
alone and unprotected—whereas the appearance of
an armed band such as theirs was might overawe
them, and show them that it was their interest to be
on friendly terms with their visitors.   Vaughan and
Roger leading the way, the men scrambled over the
rocks after them, keeping as close as they could
above the river, that, should the canoe return with
Oliver, they might not fail to see her.

Having at length surmounted the ridge, they found
themselves looking down into a broad and pleasant
valley, watered by another small rivulet, by the side
of which appeared an Indian village and a considerable number of people moving about, while a group,
in the midst of which they distinguished Oliver and
the young girl, was collected in front of the largest
wigwam.   The principal figure was an old Indian,
who by his dress, and the ornaments on his head,
they knew must be a chief. The girl was apparently
endeavouring to explain to the old chief how she
had found the young paleface.

" They see us," cried Roger, as he and Vaughan
with their men appeared on the top of the ridge;
" keep your weapons lowered, lads, we must do

nothing to alarm them. Stay here, and I will go down and make friends with the old chief—that fair damsel will, I doubt not, be on our side—they will be less likely to be alarmed by seeing one person approach alone."

As he was speaking, many of the Indians ran into their wigwams, and brought forth their bows and arrows, and other weapons. Those about the chief, however, remained perfectly quiet, merely turning their eyes in the direction of the strangers. Roger therefore advanced without any anxiety towards the chief, who stood waiting his arrival. Going up to the old man he took him by the hand, and explained in the choicest language he could command the object of his, and his companions' visit to that part of the country. The chief replied that he had gathered as much from what the girl had told him, and that he had heard some days before of the appearance of the white-faces on their shore. Roger expressed his surprise at this, when the Indian remarked that they had been seen on landing, and that their progress had been watched day after day, but as they had done no harm they had been allowed to proceed. " Our people are not fools," observed the old chief, " and we knew well that the further you proceeded into the country the more easily we could destroy you if we deemed it necessary."

Roger knew by this that the precautions he had taken had not been useless. His object being to

win over the chief, he did not boast of his power
to resist the attack; the well-armed party on the
top of the hill would produce more effect, he knew,
than anything he could say. He now turned to
Oliver and his companion. On looking at the
maiden, he had no doubt, from the form of her
features and her fair complexion, that she was of
English parentage, though not a word of English
had she uttered. His curiosity to know how she
was thus living among the Indians was very great;
on this point, however, she could give him no information. She had lived always with them, and
she believed that the old chief was her grandfather;
from the latter, therefore, only could he hope to
obtain an answer to his questions. The old chief
was, however, evidently not disposed to reply to
him; the maiden was one of their tribe, and such
she must always be, he answered at length; so
Roger saw that it would be wise not to press the
matter just then. He accordingly, feeling satisfied
with what the chief had said, asked if he knew
aught of a white man who had long been in that
region, or of two youths who had lately been
brought thither.

"Wise men do not reply till they have time to
consider the object of the questions put to them,"
answered the chief; "if you come as friends, as
friends we will receive you, and give you the best
our country affords. You may invite your companions down into the valley, they need fear no
danger."

"It is not our habit to fear danger," answered Roger, "but we have confidence in your friendship; when danger is threatened, we know how to defend ourselves." Having made this remark, which had its due effect, he hastened back to Vaughan, and after a short consultation, they agreed to accept the chief's invitation, but to keep a strict watch, in case of treachery.

CHAPTER X.

OLIVER and the young girl were, in the mean time, eagerly endeavouring to understand each other. They had left the group and were seated together on the bank of the stream. Some new ideas had evidently come into her mind; it seemed to flash upon her that she was of the same race as the young paleface by her side. She had never known a father, she said, or mother, and the squaw who had more especially tended on her in her childhood had as tawny a skin as the rest of her tribe. Now and then she talked with Oliver, but oftener sat with her finger on her brow, lost in thought. After some time she began to understand his questions better than at first. She replied that she would try to find out what he wanted to know and tell him. Oliver felt himself every instant becoming more and more interested; he could not help thinking, as he watched her varying countenance, that she must be of his own race. Perhaps her name would assist him to discover the truth. He asked, looking up in her face, what she was called.

"Manita," she answered, " does it sound pleasant in your ears ? "

"Very pleasant indeed," he replied, repeating it, " I shall remember it as long as I live."

The old chief received the adventurers in a friendly manner, and to prove his good intentions, said that he would direct his people to build wigwams for them on any spot they might choose. Roger replied that as he and his people were fond of water, they should prefer encamping on the bank of the river, where the rivulet ran into it; his true motive being that they should thus have only two sides to defend should they by any chance be attacked; while they might also, by building rafts, descend the stream into the main river and thus regain their ship.

The whole of the population at once set to work to supply the wants of the white strangers, the men even being condescending enough to assist, though the women were chiefly employed in bringing the materials for the huts and putting them up. The Englishmen, however, as soon as they saw their mode of proceeding, greatly lightened their labours. The rest of the men went out hunting, and before evening returned with a plentiful supply of game. In a wonderfully short time a village had sprung up, affording ample accommodation in fine summer weather.

After the Indians had left them, the young girl came fearlessly into their midst, bringing the fish she had caught as her present to Oliver and the two officers, for she at once distinguished them from the rest of the men. She had then a further

N

talk with Oliver ; she inquired whether he would be willing to accompany her in her canoe up the stream, and as they would have a long way to go, he must assist in paddling, but no one else must accompany them, nor must the Indians or his own friends know where they had gone. There might be some danger, she confessed, though it was not such as to make her hesitate if she could serve her new friends.

Oliver, who liked the notion of the danger, replied that he would willingly go.

She advised him to sleep soundly and to be awake two hours before dawn, when he would find her with the canoe at the mouth of the stream, beneath a high bank, from which he could easily step on board without being seen. " I will tell you more when we are away," she added, " but if any one is awake and asks where you are going, you can let them understand that you are about to fish in the stream, and my people will not be surprised, as it is my chief occupation. I have no pleasure in working with the squaws, who have little love for me, because I am the favourite of my grandfather, who allows me to do what I like."

Such, in substance, was what the young girl said to Oliver. He promised faithfully to obey her injunctions, and to be ready to accompany her at the time she had fixed on. He had some difficulty in going to sleep for thinking of the expedition he was to make on the morrow, but he at length succeeded in dropping off. After sleeping

for some time he opened his eyes, and feeling broad
awake, crept out of the hut, thinking that it was
time to set out; but as he could see the sentries at
their posts—for Roger judged it wise to place men
on the watch lest the Indians might play them
false—he waited till the one next him had moved
to the end of his beat, and then keeping under the
shade of the huts, stole down towards the river's
bank.　Moving on cautiously, he soon reached the
spot at which the girl had told him to wait for her.
Sitting down, he gazed at the stream which rippled
by in front of him, ere it joined the broad river
on his right.　The murmuring of the water as it

sounded in his
ears soon had
the not un-
usual effect of
sending him
off again to
sleep.　He
awoke with a
start on hear-
ing a gentle
voice calling
to him. Rub-
bing his eyes
as he looked
round, he saw
the shadowy
form of the
maiden stand-

ing up in her canoe, just below his feet. Forgetting its frail structure, he was about to leap
into it, when she, observing his intention, exclaimed in a louder voice than she would otherwise
have used,

" Stay, stay, or you will break through the
canoe, and put a stop to our expedition."

Oliver, taking her hand, which she extended to
him, stepped carefully into the canoe, and seated
himself at her bidding. As he did so, she turned
the canoe away from the bank, and the next instant
they were in the broader river.

" We will first steer down the stream," she whispered, " and then cross to the opposite side, lest
any one should have seen us. Take the paddle
you will find at your feet."

Oliver looked towards the shore, but could see
no one, and felt therefore satisfied that they were
not watched.

" It is well," observed Manita ; " we may therefore the sooner proceed up the stream."

In another minute they were paddling away, Manita dexterously steering the canoe. Having got
so far from the village that their voices could not be
heard, Oliver inquired the object of the expedition.

" You wish to gain news of a white man who has
been long in this country?" answered Manita ;
" when I heard what you said, I recollected that
two moons ago I had gone on an expedition up this
river with two other girls somewhat older than myself. They took me with them to steer while they

paddled. Their object was to run away from those
they did not love, and to hide in the forest till they
could return with safety. The river, though not
very wide, continues on far, far away; and we
paddled on all day; and not till night did we come
to the end of our voyage. They secured the canoe
beneath an overhanging tree, whose boughs afforded
us shelter while we slept. At daylight, leaping out
of the canoe, with their basket of provisions, and
telling me to take it back, but not to say where
they had gone, they ran off into the forest. This I
had no fancy for doing—not that I should have
been punished — but I liked not to be deceived,
and wished to know what they were about. I accordingly, instead of doing as they had bid me, followed their trail; though I kept at such a distance
that they could not hear or see me should they look
back. On they went, till I began to grow weary
and hungry; they stopped to eat, but I had forgotten to bring provisions with me, not supposing
that they would go so far. I lay concealed close
to them, till I heard them get up and go on
again; then I knew that they must be intending
to go much further. Fortunately they had left
some fruit and a piece of corn-cake, which had
slipped out of one of their baskets. I ate it as I
went along, afraid of getting far behind them.

"Leaving the forest, they went over hills and
down valleys, and up other hills; and I had great
difficulty in concealing myself—indeed, had they not
hurried on without looking back, they must have

discovered me. They now entered another forest; they were getting farther and farther from me, and I was becoming more and more weary. I was still trying to overtake them, when I felt a sharp pain in my foot—a thorn had pierced it, and sinking to the ground, I knew not what happened. How long I had thus lain I could not tell, when opening my eyes I saw a tall man, dressed in skins, but his face was fairer than that of any Indian I had ever beheld; his hair light and long; and on his head he wore a covering of straw. He cast a kind look at me, but I saw that he was as much astonished as I was at seeing him. Stooping down, he spoke some words which I did not understand; he then addressed me in Indian, and asked me who I was, and whence I had come. I told him at once that I was the grand-daughter of Oncagua, and that I was following some girls of the tribe who had run away, begging him to tell me if he knew where they were gone. He replied that they were safe with those by whom they would be better treated than they were by their own people. My foot paining me while he was speaking, I groaned, and he stooped down and pulled out the thorn, when he bound up the wound with some leaves, fastening them on with the fibres of a tree; then, seeing that I could not walk, he took me up in his arms and carried me to a dwelling larger than any I had ever before seen. It was on the borders of the forest, surrounded by a garden and corn-field; close to it, at a little distance was a large Indian village.

"He asked me if I would be content to remain there till the wound in my foot was healed. I felt sure that he would treat me kindly, though I wanted to go back to Oncagua, who would be mourning for me.

To this the white man did not object, though he said that he should have wished me to remain with him. He watched over me with the greatest care, and in three days my foot was well; and though I did not learn that which I wanted to know—what had become of my companions—I wished to go back to my grandfather. I told the strange white man this, and he would not stop me, he said, though he was loth to part with me. I, too, was grieved to part with him, for he had been very kind, and told me wonderful things about the great God who rules the world, and One who was punished instead of man, that man's sins might be forgiven, and that he might be made friends with God, and go to live with him in the sky. And he told me much more, but I could not understand it.

"When he found how much I wished to go back he said that he would go with me as far as the river, where I had left my canoe; that he should like to see me safely to my grandfather, but that he was bound by an oath to the chief with whom he lived not to go beyond the river, and that he could not break that oath, though it cost him so much. He had not allowed any of the people in the village to see me all this time, as he was afraid that they might prevent my going away. He set off with me, therefore, very early in the morning, and as I knew the way I had come from the place where he found me, I was able to lead him directly to the canoe. He was very sad at parting from me, and sighed much, and made me promise that I would come back to him again if I could. I found the canoe safe, as no one had passed that way. He asked me if I was not afraid of remaining by myself, but with a laugh I told him no; that I had often been out in the forest alone; that I would sleep in the canoe that night, and be away by dawn in the morning. Still he seemed very sorry to let me go, as he wanted to tell me more of the wonderful things about which he had spoken, and the happy country of spirits to which good men go. He said, therefore, that he would not leave me till he had seen me begin my voyage. We lighted a fire, therefore, and cooked some birds which we had shot as we came along, and then when it was time to go to sleep, while I lay down in my canoe, he climbed up into a tree above me, and lay down among the thick branches, so that he could watch me.

It was just daylight when I heard his voice telling me that it would be time for me to begin my voyage, after I had had some more food. He then kneeling down, prayed to his God to take care of me, and blessed me; and then kissing my brow, helped to force the canoe out into the stream. As I turned my head several times I saw him still standing on the bank watching me, till I could see him no longer. As the current was with me, I got back early in the day, before my grandfather and the other men who had gone out hunting had come back. None of the squaws dared to ask where I had been, nor whether any other girls had accompanied me; so I went into my grandfather's hut, and waited till he had come back.

"When he appeared, he was too glad to see me to be angry; indeed, he never has been angry with me since I can remember, but has looked upon me as above every one else in the tribe, so that I can come and go as I like. I would not say where I had been all that day, but the next I told him of my long voyage up the river, how I had hurt my foot in the woods, and had been helped by the strange white man. On hearing this, he replied that the white man must be a wicked magician; that it was he probably who had enticed the other girls away; and that, perhaps, if I went back, he would kill and eat me. I knew that this was not true, or why had he not done so at first, had he wished it?

" Since then, I have been longing to go back to see the white man; but I found that a watch was kept on me. When I heard you, however, inquiring for a white man, I at once thought that the stranger I had seen must be the one you were in search of, and I resolved to help you to find him, being assured that he is no magician."

"I have great hopes that he is the very man we are in search of," exclaimed Oliver, after Manita had finished her narrative, which took much longer time to give than it has to describe, seeing that she had to repeat it in a variety of ways before she was satisfied that her listener understood what she said. She had brought a good supply of provisions, and as Oliver hinted that he was getting very hungry, somewhere about noon she guided the canoe towards the bank, where they rested for awhile, and ate their food. They then paddled on again with renewed vigour. Manita complimented Oliver on the way in which he handled his paddle, and remarked that they were getting on much faster than when she had gone up before. It was thus some time before evening when she announced that they had arrived at the spot where she had before landed. Having run the canoe close to the bank under a tree, they secured it, and stepped on shore.

"We will take some provisions with us this time," she observed, "for though I may kill some birds with my arrows, it will delay us to do so."

They set off at once, and made good progress before sunset, when, at Oliver's suggestion, they both climbed up into a tree, in which he formed a sort of platform, where she could sleep securely; he afterwards making another for himself. They set off again at dawn, and Oliver, helping Manita over the rough hills, to which he, a Devonshire lad, was well accustomed, they made good progress. At last the clearing Manita had described was reached, and they saw before them the white man standing in front of his dwelling.

"There he is!" exclaimed Manita. "Oh, I am

so glad to see him !" and she bounded on ahead of
Oliver.   The recluse, for such he seemed, welcomed Manita affectionately, but his gaze was
turned towards Oliver.   "Who are you, young
sir?" he exclaimed, looking from one to the other
of his visitors.

"Oliver Dane, sir, from near Dartmouth, in
Devonshire," he answered.

The recluse appeared greatly agitated. "Speak,
speak: with whom came you? when did you reach
this distant land?" he asked.

"I arrived here five days since, sir," replied
Oliver, "in the *Rainbow*, commanded by Captain

Layton, with Master Roger Layton, Master Vaughan Audley, and a company of twenty men."

" Vaughan Audley !" exclaimed the recluse; "is he with you?"

" He is with the rest of the party, thirty miles or more away down the river," answered Oliver.

" And Mistress Audley, and her daughter Lettice—can you give me tidings of them?" continued the recluse, before Oliver had finished his reply.

" I left Mistress Audley and Lettice at James Town a week since," answered Oliver; "but, alack ! Gilbert and young Fenton were carried off by the Indians, and we have come up in search of them, as we have of Captain Audley; and, if I mistake not, sir, you are that very gentleman."

" I am indeed so; I believed that I was long ago supposed to be dead," answered Captain Audley "or that search would have been made for me."

Oliver then told him all he knew respecting the report brought home by Batten. " But how comes it that my son did not accompany Manita?" inquired Captain Audley.

" She will tell you why she would only bring me," answered Oliver. Manita's reply seemed to satisfy him; he then made many eager inquiries about Gilbert, as to whom and by whom he had been carried off. Oliver gave him all the information in his power. So interested had he been, that he had forgotten to invite the young travellers into his house ; he now, however, did so, and placed before them an ample meal. Manita seemed somewhat puzzled how to behave, but looking at Oliver she imitated him very well. Their host frequently gazed at the young people, as he plied Oliver further with questions.

"When will you come with us, sir?" asked Oliver, after waiting for some time; "Manita is, I know, in a hurry to get back, and all will be ready to welcome you when you arrive."

"Alas! I cannot go thus far unless one who holds my pledge is ready to set me free," answered Captain Audley. "He may be willing to do so, or fear of the white man's power may induce him to release me."

"I suppose, sir, you would not object to be carried off by force, if the Indians will not by fair means let you go free?" said Oliver.

"As to that I shall make no answer, lad," replied Captain Audley; "I wish by fair means alone to gain my liberty. I have, though, another motive for remaining : to search, with the aid of my Indian friends, for my boy Gilbert and his companions, who have been brought, you say, by their captors to this part of the country. I will therefore bid you return and invite the party to come up here. Their presence will, I hope, have its effect."

The recluse, or Captain Audley, for such it appeared that he was, continued looking at his young guests; suddenly turning to Oliver, he asked whether he had heard that he had a sister born

some short time before the settlement was de-
stroyed.

"Yes," answered Oliver, "my mother had a
little daughter named Virginia, the first child born
in the settlement, who was, my grandfather supposed, murdered with her and my father on that
cruel day."

"It may have been so," remarked Captain
Audley, "but she may have escaped; and the
thought occurred to me when I first saw this little
damsel; for a child of white parents she un-
doubtedly is, though brought up with Indian ways
and manners; and when I saw you and her together and heard your name, judging by your age,
and on examining your countenances, which
strongly resemble each other, I at once became
impressed with the idea that she was no other than
Virginia Dane, and therefore your sister. There
was no other child in the settlement so young as
she must have been when it was attacked, and
none so likely to have had its life spared."

Oliver looked upon Manita with still greater
interest than before, and giving her a kiss, told her
what the white man had said, and asked her
whether she would wish to be his sister.

"Yes, yes," she answered, with a look of
pleasure; "and you will come and live at our village, and go out fishing and hunting with me, and
become some day chief of our tribe."

Oliver tried to explain that it was much more
fitting that she should come and live among the

English. At first she did not understand this, and doubted whether her grandfather would allow her to go. Oliver had then to explain that the old chief was not her grandfather ; possibly, that he or his followers had murdered their parents, though for some reason he had saved her life. This seemed to make her waver ; she promised Oliver that she would consider the matter.

" You are too weary to return at once, my young guests," observed Captain Audley. " While you rest, I will go to the village that you see yonder and seek out the chief Wamsutah. I may be able to win him over to assist in our object. I trust by means of the influence I possess over his mind, to induce him to aid in the recovery of my son Gilbert and his companion. He possesses more power than any chief of the neighbouring tribes, Powhattan excepted ; and should he learn where they are to be found, he will not fail to obtain their release."

Saying this, Captain Audley took his departure, leaving Oliver and Manita in his dwelling. A considerable time passed, however, before he returned. Manita, overcome with fatigue, had fallen asleep in a corner of the room, wrapped up in her cloak. Oliver was too anxious to close his eyes. As he watched the features of the young girl, he felt more and more convinced that the surmise of Captain Audley was correct, and he thought of the happiness it would be to restore her to civilized life, and of the blessing she might prove to their aged grandfather, whom she might tend with a watchful care far better than he was able to bestow. At last he too dropped off asleep. He was awakened by the return of their host.

"Have you succeeded, sir?" he asked, eagerly.

"I have news of the two lads, who are many hours' journey from this, in the hands of a tribe, alas! at enmity with Wamsutah and his people. I cannot hope, consequently, to communicate with them without much difficulty, and must wait an opportunity, which I pray God to afford me. I would have you, therefore, after resting here to-night, hasten back to your people; tell my son Vaughan how I long to embrace him, but that stern necessity compels me to remain here awhile, till the chief permits me to depart with honour, and I can bring back the two missing ones. I do not advise Vaughan and Master Layton to come up here, lest they should create suspicion in the minds of the Indians. Let them be on their guard against treachery, which this people look upon more as a virtue than a crime; and if they can obtain canoes from the chief Oncagua, or can contrive to build them, let them by all means return down the river, which they will find navigable to the mouth. They would thus avoid many dangers through which they before unconsciously passed, and regain the ship far more speedily than by land."

Oliver promised to deliver the messages he had received from Captain Audley, who the next morning told him that he had provided two Indian lads, his pupils, in whom he could implicitly trust to escort him and Manita to the canoe. Setting off, they safely reached it, and anxious to arrive at the village before night, at once paddled briskly down the stream. It was dark, however, before they neared their destination, and Manita proposed that they should land at the English village. As they approached they were hailed by Ben Tarbox from the bank, to whom Oliver replied.

"Thankful to hear your voice, Master Dane," said Ben, as he helped them out of the canoe, which he drew up on the bank. "We thought you were lost, and the old chief has been in a great taking about his granddaughter, accusing us of spiriting her away, and well-nigh creating a breach of the peace."

"We have not been on a fool's errand, Ben," answered Oliver. "I want to speak to our commander without delay, wherever he is."

"He and Master Audley are on foot, for we don't know at what moment the natives may take it into their fickle heads to attack us," answered Ben. "Here they come."

Oliver, followed by Manita, hastened to meet Vaughan and Roger, and as fast he could pour out his words, he told them of his adventure. Vaughan, prompted by filial affection, was eager to set off to meet his father, but Oliver reminded him of the advice he had brought that the party should remain at their present post, and Roger also giving his opinion to the same effect, he agreed to wait further tidings. They might, however, be compelled to move for want of provisions, though their present stock would enable them to remain some days longer, but a small portion having been exhausted. They had hopes, too, that when Oncagua should discover that Manita was safe, his confidence would be restored, and that he would be as ready as at first to supply them with food. Both Vaughan and Roger agreed that the likeness between Manita and Oliver was very great, and they had little doubt that she was really Captain White's grandchild. Oliver declared that he had no doubt about the matter, and already felt towards her as a brother for a sister. She by this time fully comprehended that she was of the white man's race, and when Vaughan asked her if she would go back to Oncagua, she burst into tears.

No, she replied; she would remain with her new brother. The chief was generally kind, but he might keep her prisoner or send her off further away, when she could not return to her brother.

There might be truth in what the maiden said; and though they hoped, by her means, to restore a good understanding between themselves and Oncagua, they would not deliver her up into his power. It was agreed, therefore, that she should remain in the village during the night.

Oliver begged that he might go the next morning to the chief, and tell him how matters had fallen out.

" A brave thought," exclaimed Vaughan. " You shall go, and when the chief sees you he will be convinced that you speak the truth."

Next morning Oliver set out, with his sword by his side, which, young as he was, he knew how to use; but without other arms. The Indians gazed at him as he walked fearlessly on till he reached the wigwam of the chief, who had just come forth. In the best language he could command he delivered his message, and then told him that he was the brother of her whom he had so long nourished and protected, and that he came to thank him for the kindness he had shown her; that she was now with her own people, who heartily desired to be the friends of On-cagua and his tribe.

The chief gazed at the bold youth with astonishment. "Does she remain willingly with them, or do they keep her as a prisoner?" he asked.

"It is of her own free will that she remains," answered Oliver.

The chief

sighed; "It is true that her parents were pale-faces," he said, " but the heart of Oncagua yearns towards her, and he has ever regarded her as his child."

"But our grandfather has no other descendants than us two, and his heart will be made glad when he hears that the daughter of his only child is alive," replied Oliver; "it may be that Oncagua remembers the chief of the palefaces when they first settled at Roanoke, Massey White."

"He was my friend, my brother," answered the old chief; "it was for his sake, in return for the kindness he did me, that I saved his grandchild, and would have saved her mother had I possessed the means of carrying her off. Though I shall grieve to lose the maiden, yet willingly will I send her to him to cheer his declining years. Bring her to me; she need not fear that I will detain her; but I will gaze at her once again before you take her away with you to your distant home. For her sake you and your companions may rest assured that Oncagua will remain, as he has ever been, a friend to the palefaces."

Highly satisfied with the result of his embassy, Oliver hastened back to the camp. After due consultation Vaughan and Roger agreed to allow Virginia, if she was so minded, to accompany Oliver to the chief; should they not do so, it might show want of confidence, and Oliver declared that he would die fighting for her sooner than allow her to

be carried off. She at first hesitated, but when
Oliver told her what the chief had said, she consented to accompany him. Holding each other
fast by the hand they set out, no one even address-
ing them till they reached the chief's wigwam.
Oncagua stood at the entrance waiting for them;
he gazed with a fond look at the young girl for
some minutes without speaking.

"Do you leave me willingly?" he asked at
length, in a tone of grief. She burst into tears.
"Had I not found my white brother, I would have
remained with you, and tended you in sickness
and old age," she said, "but now I desire to go
where he goes, and to dwell with those of my own
colour."

"Go, my child, go, the Great Spirit will have it
so—and when you are far away, Oncagua will dream
that you are happy with those of your own kindred
and race." As he spoke, he entered his wigwam;
quickly returning with a small package carefully
done up in opossum skin. "Take this with you,"
he said, "it contains the clothes you wore and the
chain you bore round your neck as an infant; it
will prove to your grandfather that you are indeed
his daughter's child." Taking the maiden in his
arms, he pressed her to his heart, and then placing
her hand in that of Oliver, told him to hasten back
to his friends, as if he doubted his own resolution
to give her up. The rest of the people, who had
collected from all sides, gazed on the paleface maiden

and her brother, with glances of admiration and awe, regarding them as beings of a superior nature to themselves.

Vaughan and Roger were on the watch to welcome them back; they both felt that they could not sufficiently thank the young maiden for the service she had done them, and they wished to express to Oliver their sense of his courage and boldness.

"I have done nothing that I should be thanked," said Virginia, for by her rightful name they now called her; "I heard that you were in search of a white man, and knowing where one was to be found, I took my brother to him."

The object of their expedition, however, was not yet accomplished; they knew that Captain Audley was alive, but he and their two friends were still a long way off, and it might be a hard matter to reach them. Two days passed by, and they were becoming impatient, for as their stock of provisions was now growing short, they must depend on the Indians for their supply, and should they refuse it, they would be entirely in their power. Virginia and Oliver offered to make another expedition up the river to communicate with Captain Audley, but Vaughan considered himself bound to abide by his father's commands. Roger proposed that they should instead borrow the maiden's canoe, which still lay on the bank, and send down to the ship. Oliver at once offered to go, and suggested that Ben Tarbox, who

knew well how to handle a canoe, should be asked
to accompany him.

" Of course I will," answered Ben, " if it was six
times as far. We'll find our way down easily enough,
and if the navigation is clear, we'll come back in the
long-boat, and bring a good store of provision and
arms, and a couple of swivels in the bows in case we
fall in with any Indians likely to give us a taste of
their arrows."

It was of course necessary to consult Virginia
about taking her canoe. On hearing that Oliver was
going, she insisted on going also ; she understood
better than any one else how to manage the canoe,
and she was eager to see the big ship and the good
captain who had known her father. So determined
was she that Vaughan and Roger had to yield, believing that with so careful a man as Tarbox she
would not be exposed to more danger than by remaining with them. As soon as the arrangement
was made, she hastened to the canoe, which she
examined thoroughly, covering the seams afresh
with a gummy substance, a lump of which she produced from the bow. She also found a third paddle,
which, she observed, would be for the sailor's use.
As the day was far spent, it was necessary to wait
till the next morning. Virginia was up before daybreak, and summoning Oliver and Ben, announced
that it was time to start, that they might not be seen
by the Indians, who might perchance wish to stop
them. Vaughan and Roger with some of the men,

came down to see them off. Ben, who sat in the bow, had his musket by his side; Oliver paddled next to him, and Virginia, who seemed to consider herself as captain of the craft, sat in the stern and steered. Their friends uttering a prayer for their safety, they pushed off from the bank, and commenced their voyage.

CHAPTER XI

THE young maiden steered the canoe in a way which excited Ben's warmest admiration. The roar of the rapids was soon heard ahead; not a moment did she hesitate; onward sped the canoe, straight as an arrow. Moving her paddle now on one side, now on the other, she guided it down the steep descent, the water bubbling and foaming, the tops of the

dark rocks appearing on either side, against which had the frail fabric struck it must have been dashed to pieces. Even Ben held in his breath till they were once more in smooth water.

"Paddle on! paddle on!" she cried; and Oliver repeated the order to Ben, who understood not her language. A wall of trees rose on either bank, above which the blue sky appeared, tinged with the light of morning, though the stream down which the canoe sped her way still lay in deepest gloom. Every rock and sand-bank was well known to Virginia, who steered steadily onward. Gradually the stream widened, and the current ran with less force. Hitherto, scarcely a word had been uttered, except when the young pilot directed her crew to cease paddling or to paddle on.

"How shall we be able to get up in the long-boat?" asked Oliver, who thought that he might at length venture to speak; "nearly as much water is required as a man could wade through."

Virginia understood his explanation. "There is another passage to the left, where the water is deep, though the current is rapid, and strong men can drag up such a canoe as you describe," she answered.

"Our men will not be prevented from coming up on that account, then," he remarked, satisfied that the undertaking might be accomplished.

Sooner than he expected the canoe entered the broad river, at the mouth of which he hoped to find the ship at anchor. The sun had now risen, his bright rays glancing across the placid water, which

shone like a sheet of burnished gold. Virginia gazed
at it with astonishment. " I can be your pilot no
longer," she said, " for I have been here twice only
before—the first time the water was dark and
troubled, and I thought that I had reached the
mighty lake across which the canoes of the palefaces,
as I had heard, sail from their own lands. I came
again, when seeing the opposite bank, I knew that
I was in another river, but feared to venture far lest
I should be unable to return against the current."

" Continue to steer, I pray you," said Oliver,
" Ben will act as pilot to tell you which way to go,
for neither of us can manage the canoe as you do ;
all we have to do is to keep near to the shore on
our right, and we cannot miss our way."

Virginia seemed well pleased at the confidence
placed in her, and Oliver and Ben paddled on right
merrily. Though the river was so broad, there still
might be shoals and rocks or sunken trees ; and
Virginia kept her gaze ahead, to be ready to avoid
them or any other dangers. The current having
less strength than in the smaller stream, the canoe
did not make as rapid way as at first ; still, as they
looked at the trees on the right, they saw that they
were going at a speed with which no ordinary boat
could compete.

As midday drew on, Oliver proposed landing to
take their meal, but to this Virginia objected, as
there might be inhabitants on the shore, who might
come suddenly upon them before they had time to
embark. They therefore took such food as they

required, allowing the canoe meantime to float down. Virginia had not failed to look out for any canoe which might dart out upon them, for, taught by experience, she knew that they were more likely to contain foes than friends. None, however, appeared.

The sun was already sinking astern when Ben announced that he recognized the mouth of the river, and as they rounded a point, he shouted, " Hurrah ! there's the ship all right—we shall soon be aboard and astonish them not a little."

They were hailed as they approached by the sentry on the forecastle, who seeing the maiden in her Indian dress, knew not what to expect. Ben's reply assured him who they were, and Captain Layton and the rest of the crew quickly gathered at the side to help Virginia upon deck. She hesitated for a moment ; the huge ship astonished her, surpassing all her imaginings. On hearing from Oliver who she was, the captain endeavoured by every sign he could make to show his satisfaction. " Tell her," he said to Oliver, " that I knew her father, a brave Christian man, and she shall be to me as a daughter, so that she shall never regret the Indian friends she has left."

He kissed her brow as he spoke, and she seemed at once to understand him. He then led her down into the cabin, round which she looked with a gaze of astonishment at the numberless articles, so strange to her eyes. " Tell her we cannot yet turn her into an English girl, for Cicely has left none of her clothes on board, and they would not fit her slim figure if she had," said Captain Layton, "but in the mean time she must learn English, and when we get back to James Town we will rig her out properly, and she will soon be able to talk her native tongue— though I don't suppose she ever spoke much of it in early life."

The captain had, however, but little time just then to attend to Virginia, as Oliver had further to explain the condition of the party, and to beg that the long-boat might be sent up to their assistance. As she, however, had been waiting all this time for the return of the party, it was necessary to send for her, and she could not arrive till nightfall. Oliver and Ben volunteered to go for her at once ; though they had been paddling all day, a few hours more work would do them no harm. Virginia wanted to accompany them when she heard they were going, but this the captain would not allow. Though she seemed very unhappy at parting from her brother, Oliver soothed her by assuring her that he would soon be back ; and slipping into the canoe, he and Ben set off.

"Well, I never was at sea in a craft like this before, its planking not much thicker than a sheet of paper," said Ben, as they paddled on; "however, provided the water keeps out, it matters little whether the planking is three inches or the tenth of an inch thick."

They paddled on and on, keeping as close into the beach as they could venture; Ben observing, it would not do to run the risk of touching a rock or sandbank either. The tide, on which they had not calculated, was against them, as was a light breeze, so that they were longer than they expected in reaching the bay where they had landed. It was then growing dusk, and as they looked towards the shore, they saw several figures running down. A musket-ball came whistling not far from their ears; on this Ben shouted pretty lustily. They paddled on as fast as they could to the boat; she lay, contrary to orders, close to the beach.

"Pretty fellows you are, to shoot at your friends," exclaimed Ben.

"We took you for natives," answered one of the men, "and thought it might be that you were coming to carry off the boat."

"If you had been where you ought to have been —on board her—they would have found that a hard job," replied Ben.

"We were only stretching our legs, Master Tarbox, while we looked out for the rest. What has become of them?" asked the man.

"You'll have to stretch your arms now, mates," said Ben; "and I'll tell you all about that as we go along."

The long-boat was quickly shoved off, and the canoe being fastened astern, Oliver took the helm, and the crew gave way with a will, glad enough to return to the ship. Ben then told them that they would have a much longer pull on the morrow, and as he hoped attain the object of their expedition.

Such a trip, in spite of the hard work they would have to go through, not free from danger though it might be, was exactly to their tastes.

They reached the ship two hours after dark. The captain had been getting ready provisions and ammunition so that they might start at dawn of day. Virginia, surmising their intentions, crept out of the cabin, and was on the watch, intending to go also. Oliver had no little difficulty in persuading her to remain, and not till he told her that the great chief who commanded the big canoe would not allow her to go did she consent to remain. A light breeze blowing up the river, the long-boat, with the canoe astern, sped merrily on her voyage. Oliver had taken care to obtain from his sister, as far as he could understand her language, an exact description of the channel by which the rapids might be avoided. With a strong current against them, heavy also as the boat was, they made much slower progress during the second part. They were still some way from the rapids when night overtook them. Oliver and Ben agreed that it would be impossible to attempt the channel unless in broad daylight; they therefore secured their boat to the bank under a wide-spreading tree.

Oliver, young as he was, knew the importance of being on their guard against surprise. Accordingly he and Ben searched round to ascertain whether any Indians were lurking in the neighbourhood; he also stationed a sentry on shore with orders to keep his ears open, that he might give timely notice of the approach of a foe. The night passed off, however, without interruption.

"Now, lads, we must get up these rapids before the hot sun comes down to make the toil harder to bear," cried Ben, rousing the men up. "For the next three or four miles the water is deep and free from rocks, as I noted when we came down, and we may get along it in the twilight."

Ben was right, and, with the early light, the rapids came in sight ahead; then, steering to the right, they found the channel Virginia had described. The depth at the entrance was sufficient to float the boat, but it was too narrow to allow the oars to be worked. The only way, therefore, by which they could hope to get on was to land and tow the boat up against the current. This was no easy matter, as in many places the stems and roots of the trees came close down to the water's edge, while the wide branches formed a thick canopy overhead. Still, sometimes pulling, at others wading, and at others landing and towing on the boat, they hoped by perseverance to succeed. While thus engaged they knew that, should any hostile natives attack them, they must be taken at a woeful disadvantage. The arms therefore were placed in the boat, so that each one might seize his weapon in an instant, while two men proceeded as scouts through the forest on the right to give warning should a foe approach. Thus, after an hour's toil they emerged into the broad stream, some way above the rapids, when they were able once more to take to their oars.

Oliver judged that Virginia had avoided this passage when they descended, as the darkness in which it must have been plunged at that time would have prevented her from seeing the way, while the danger to her slight canoe from the roots projecting into the water and the sunken logs would have been far greater than that from the rocks of the rapids.

CHAPTER XII.

E must now go back to the moment when Gilbert and Fenton, anxious to obtain some venison for themselves and their hungry companions, were creeping along in the hopes of getting a shot at the deer they had seen from the fort. Having at length, as they supposed, got close enough to the deer to make sure of it, Gilbert was on the point of firing when, hearing Fenton cry out, he looked round and saw his friend, to his dismay, in the hands of several Indians; while others, springing forward, seized his arms before he could even point his gun towards them.

It was useless, they knew, to plead for mercy; the Indians, indeed, threatened them by signs with instant death should they cry out.

They were hurried on at a rapid rate till they reached a ford across the stream, which ran as they supposed by their camp. On and on they went, six only of their captors remaining with them, while the main body returned into the forest.

" They cannot go on for ever," observed Gilbert, " and as they must camp at some time or other, we must then look out for an opportunity to escape. It would be a shame to our manhood were we to allow ourselves to be held captive by six Indians."

"I am ready for any plan you may propose,"
answered Fenton, "but it will be no easy matter to
get free without weapons and with our arms secured
behind our backs."

"If they leave us together to-night, I will try
what my teeth can do," answered Gilbert, "in
casting loose the bonds which bind your hands, and
you can then render the same good service to me."

"I pray that we may have the chance," remarked
Fenton, "though, when our arms are free, how we
are to escape from the lynx-eyed natives I know
not."

"That must be as opportunity offers," said
Gilbert.

The possibility of escaping kept up their
spirits, and they moved along with apparent willingness in the direction the Indians wished them
to go. They had thus made considerable progress
before nightfall, when the Indians halted in a small
open space in the midst of a thick wood, where
they lighted a fire and prepared, as it seemed, to
pass the night there. Much to Gilbert and Fenton's disappointment, however, the cunning natives
placed them apart, one on each side of the fire,
though they gave them to eat some of the venison
and dried fish which they carried in their wallets.

"We must put a good face on the matter, and
not let them suspect our intentions," observed
Gilbert. "Let us sing them a merry stave. It will

make them fancy we are thoughtless about the future, and they will deem it less necessary to watch us closely. No matter the words, provided the tune is such as to take their fancy."

Thereon they struck up an air which they had often sung on board ship. The Indians nodded their heads approvingly. Next morning two of the Indians went out hunting, and on their return with a small deer, shared the flesh with their prisoners. After this they travelled on as before, and continued moving to the northward for two more days. Every mile they went they felt that their chance of escape was lessening, still, like brave lads, they did not give way to despair. They tried to learn from the Indians what had become of their party; they understood that they were on a war-path, but would ere long overtake them.

"To-night or never we must make our attempt to escape, Ned," said Gilbert. "I have heard tell of the cruel tricks of these Indians, who only spare the lives of their prisoners at first, that they may carry them to their villages to show them to their squaws, before they put them to death with the most cruel tortures. Such may be the lot they intend for us, and such an ending is not to my taste any more than it is to yours, I am sure."

"That it is not," said Fenton; "and if we can once free our arms and get hold of our weapons, we may, at all events, have a brave tussle for life."

Another night came. Gilbert lay down some way farther off from the fire than usual, and Fenton,

pretending to stumble as he passed, threw himself
down by his side. Their guards, taking no notice
of this, allowed them to remain where they were,
while they set themselves to cooking part of a deer
they had shot during the day. The Indians, who
had been ranging two at a time over the country in
search of game, were more tired than usual, and
after gorging themselves with venison, lay down to
sleep, one only remaining on guard to keep up the
fire. He, too, after piling on more wood, which,
being green, did not blaze up, sat down, and in a
short time Gilbert saw him stretch himself at his
length, a loud snore announcing that he, also, had
gone to sleep. Gilbert had been gradually getting
his head
closer and
closer to Fen-
ton's arms;
he now in
eager haste
began to
gnaw away at
the leathern
thongs which
bound them.
The task was
not an easy
one, and such
as a sailor
only, accus-
tomed to all

sorts of knots, could have accomplished. It was done at length, when, lifting up his head, he observed that the Indians were still fast asleep. Fenton on this, slowly rolling round, with his hands at liberty, quickly cast off Gilbert's bonds. To get hold of their weapons was their next task. Fortunately, their fire-arms and ammunition-belts had been carried by the Indians who lay nearest to them; they marked this while the fire was still blazing, and therefore knew where to find them. While Fenton crawled towards one, Gilbert in the same way approached the other,—now stooping, now moving a few inches, till he felt his hands on his weapon. Fenton eagerly grasping his sword, rose to his feet, and drawing it from its scabbard, pointing Gilbert to do the same, made as if he would kill the sleeping Indians. Gilbert lifted up his hand to implore him to desist just as his weapon was about to descend, scarcely able to refrain from crying out. Fenton obeyed him. He then signed to him that they must next, if possible, possess themselves of the Indians' bows. The attempt was a daring one, but they so lay that they could be lifted without disturbing their owners. Though they could not carry them off, the fire would render them useless. And now, seeing how soundly the Indians slept, they lifted them one after the other, and drove their ends among the burning embers. The Indians' tomahawks were in their belts, or they would have treated them in the same manner. Any further delay would be dangerous: stooping down so that, should either of the Indians awake, there might be less chance of their being seen, they made their way into the forest. Should they keep to the south they might meet their approaching foes. They therefore turned to the east, hoping thus either to make their way to the sea or to reach the village of some friendly tribe. Every instant they expected to be pursued ; but as they stopped to listen no sound reached their ears, and they continued their course, guided by the stars, of which they could occasionally catch sight amid the openings in the trees. Should they once get to a distance, they had hopes that the Indians would not discover their trail till the morning, which would give them a long start. After going some distance they gained the open country, across which they could make their way without difficulty. Their spirits raised with the feeling of regained liberty, and the thoughts of escaping the cruel death or galling captivity which would have been their lot, they sped on.

Daylight at length broke; the rising sun now served them as a guide, and they were pushing on with his rays in their eyes, faint from their exertions, when they saw before them a broad river, on the opposite side of which, with a wood beyond, appeared an Indian village, hitherto unperceived. Descending the hill full in view of the village, they must they knew be seen. Making a virtue of necessity, Gilbert proposed that they should at once boldly enter the village and demand the hospitality of its inhabitants. A canoe lay on the bank: stepping into it, they paddled across to a landing-place, near which already a number of women and children and a few men were collected, wondering who the paleface strangers could be. Gilbert stepped boldly on shore, followed by Fenton.

" We have come as friends," he shouted, "and our wish is to be at peace with you, and with all the children of this country. Conduct us to your chief."

The bold bearing of the two youths and their good looks produced a favourable effect on the gentler portion of the inhabitants, who crowded round them, eager to examine them more nearly; whereat Gilbert and his companion smiled and offered their hands, making every sign they could think of to show their friendly feelings. At this the women looked well pleased, and inquired whether they were hungry.

" Indeed we are, fair dames," answered Fenton, making signs, " and thankful should we be for any food you can bring us."

On this several of the younger women hurried to their wigwams and soon returned with a supply of fish and plantains and several fruits, which they placed on the grass in a shady spot under a tree before the strangers, who set to with a good will, nodding right and left in acknowledgment to their entertainers. They had just finished when they saw an old Indian, whom they knew by his dress to be a chief, accompanied by several councillors, approaching them. They rose and advanced to meet him, Gilbert, who spoke the Indian language better than his companion, shouting out that they were glad to see so renowned a chief, whose friendship they desired to make. The chief, who it appeared had heard rumours of the fresh arrival of the English in the country, supposing that they were to be followed by a large army, treated them accordingly with much courtesy and respect, and assured them that everything in his village was at their disposal, and that it would be his pride to entertain them as long as they remained.

Thus far they believed that they were safe. They, however, had fears that the Indians from whom they had escaped might follow on their trail, and come to demand them. They therefore proposed, after resting, to set out again, hoping in course of time to reach the sea. The old chief, however, though he made them welcome, had no intention of letting them depart. When the next day they expressed a wish to continue their journey, he made the excuse that enemies were abroad who might take their lives, and as they were his guests that the blame would rest with him. They had expected before this the arrival of the Indians from whom they had escaped; but as another day passed by and they did not appear, they guessed truly that the tribes were at enmity, and that their captors had not dared to pursue them. It was, however, probable that they might be lurking in the neighbourhood, in the hopes of overtaking them should they venture from the village; they therefore, with less unwillingness than they would otherwise have felt, consented to remain, hoping every day that the chief would send an escort with them to the coast, which they supposed was at no great distance. When, however, they made the request to him, he observed that it was many days' journey off, and that the inhabitants were enemies, who would attack his people should he send them. Thus day after day, and week after week went by; and so strictly watched were they that they could find no opportunity of escaping. They were treated all the time, however, by the women as kindly as at first; and the chief's two daughters gave them to understand, that, if they would promise to remain, they should become their husbands and leaders of the tribe. Neither Gilbert nor Fenton, however, desired this honour, though they were too wise directly to refuse the proposal.

Their captivity being light, they were tolerably happy, and would have been more so had they been able to let their friends know that they were safe. At last, the chief confided to them the cause of their detention: a tribe, between whom and his people an hereditary feud had existed, had of late years always proved victorious, the reason being, as he observed, that they had a white man dwelling among them, who, although he did not himself fight, always directed their counsels; and now, as he had got two white men, he hoped to beat his enemies, especially if they accompanied him to battle, which he had made up his mind that they should do. On receiving this announcement, Gilbert and Fenton consulted together as to how they should act. Gilbert declared he had no wish to fight any Indians who had not molested him. As to that, Fenton thought that there was no great harm, and that it was their duty to help those who had befriended them. "If the Indians go out to fight, and we are compelled to accompany them, we may as well help them to gain the victory, and bring the war sooner to a conclusion," he answered. His reasoning, however, did not satisfy Gilbert.

"Have you considered who the white man possibly is of whom the chief speaks?" he asked. "My idea is, that, if he has been among them for several years, he must be my father; and, if so, I would never consent to fight against his friends, though he himself were not in the battle."

"I should say, on the contrary," said Fenton. "Supposing the white man spoken of is your father, they must have detained him against his will, and therefore, if we can conquer them, we shall be doing him good service by setting him free."

The next day there was a great stir in the village, and warriors from all directions came flocking in, adorned with war-paint and feathers. The chief made them a long harangue, and informed

them that his white sons were going forth with
their lightning-makers to assist them in fighting
their foes, and that victory was certain. As Gilbert still hesitated, the chief told him very plainly
that go he must or take the consequences; so,
Fenton having agreed to help the chief, he resolved
to make the best of a bad matter. He and Fenton
also intended to try and learn the whereabouts of
the white man and to protect him, whoever he was,
from their friends.

The whole force which had been marshalled over-
night set forth some hours before daylight—not
marching like an English army, shoulder to
shoulder, but following each other in several lines,
each headed by a warrior of renown, like so many
snakes stealing along the grass. Gilbert and
Fenton followed in the march, one behind the
other. Thus they proceeded across the country;
the lines never interfering with, but always keeping
in sight of, each other. At night they encamped
round several fires, a strong guard keeping watch
over those who slept. They hoped, before the
evening of the next day, to reach the territory of
their enemies. The following evening, after a short
rest in a thick forest, where no fires were lighted
which might betray them, they again set forward,
expecting ere long to come upon a village, which
they hoped to take by surprise and put all the inhabitants to death.

" I will not assist them in so horrible a butchery,"

said Gilbert; " but perchance while they are engaged in it we may find an opportunity of escaping
and letting the white man know the danger he and
his friends are in."

The Indians now advanced more cautiously even
than before, taking advantage of all the shelter
the country afforded till night came on, when,
after going some distance, a sign from the chief
was passed from line to line. They halted in a
thick wood, where they lay down, not a word being
uttered, Gilbert and Fenton following their example. As they thus lay in perfect silence, they
heard human voices, the laughter of young people,
the barking of dogs, and other sounds, coming,
evidently, from the village to be attacked. Soon
the voices died away as the inhabitants went to
rest. The night passed by, the Indians watching
eagerly for the signal to advance. It was given
about an hour before dawn, when the band of warriors crept rapidly forward like tigers about to
spring on their prey. Gilbert felt much inclined to
fire off his piece to give the doomed inhabitants the
alarm, but he feared that he and Fenton would
lose their lives; and that the inhabitants, not
having time to collect for their defence, would still
be put to death. As they approached, the lines
separated till the entire village was surrounded,
when the silence of night was broken by a succession of fearful war-whoops, and the warriors
rushed forward to their work of destruction. At

222 THE SETTLERS :

that moment, Gilbert plucking Fenton by the arm, they bounded off, unperceived by the old chief or the rest with him, their only aim being to escape from the scene of slaughter. On they went at a rate which would have made it difficult even for the Indians to overtake them. Day was breaking when they found themselves close to a river; as they glanced for an instant back, they could see the flames ascending from the burning village, round which the work of slaughter was going forward. As they could have done nothing to prevent it, it only incited them to fresh exertions to escape from the power of the savages. Happily the darkness would prevent their trail being followed, even should their escape be discovered, which it was not likely to be for some time, engaged as the Indians were ; while, in the neighbourhood of the village, it would probably be obliterated by the feet of the inhabitants who might have attempted to escape.

By following the course of the river, they hoped to meet with a canoe, of which they would not scruple to take possession. If not, Gilbert proposed that they should build a raft, to which they would rather trust themselves, imperfectly constructed as it might be, than to the tender mercies of the savages.

" For my part I would rather swim for it," cried Fenton.

" We might throw them off the scent by so doing," said Gilbert; " but then we should lose our arms or damage our powder; let us keep that dry, and be able to fight like men for our lives if need be."

"You are right, Gilbert," answered his companion; "you see we have clear ground ahead, we may make play over it."

They bounded on across a wide meadow which skirted the river for some distance, hoping that they might not be discovered till they had gained the shelter of the forest beyond. Never, probably, had they run so fast; the hope of securing their liberty gave wings to their feet, while as yet they felt able to continue their flight for many a mile more. How many they had accomplished they were unable to calculate, but at length they were compelled to stop for want of breath. Throwing themselves on the ground, they lay listening attentively for any sound which might betoken the approach of pursuers, but except the notes of the song-birds, and the harsher screams of the wild-fowl as they skimmed along the banks, nothing could they hear, and after resting for a few minutes they again, with renewed strength, sped onwards. Still, as they ran, they looked for a canoe, but none could they discover.

"We shall have to build a raft, after all," said Gilbert; "but no matter, if it will float us we will manage to get down to the sea, and then make our way along the shore till we reach the mouth of the James River."

"Let us first get beyond the reach of our late friends," answered Fenton; "it would not be safe to stop as yet, for, depend on it, they will pursue us if they once discover our trail."

Gilbert agreeing with this, they sped on as before. The country before them was again partially open, here and there interspersed with clumps of trees and copses, where the depth of soil allowed their growth.

They had just passed through a small wood when they saw before them a tall figure proceeding in the same direction in which they were going, but far more leisurely. "Can it be an Indian?" exclaimed Fenton, placing his hand on Gilbert's arm for a moment as they stopped to observe him.

"He wears a dress of skins and mocassins; he has a quiver on his back, and bow in his hand," observed Gilbert.

"Yes," replied Fenton, "but no Indian has his head covered with a hat like that, and see, if I mistake not, he has a sword girded to his side, such as an Indian never carries."

"Then let us overtake him," exclaimed Gilbert; "should he prove to be an enemy, we are two to one, we need not fear him, although my hope is that he is a friend."

"On, then," cried Fenton, and, setting off, they quickly gained on the stranger. Hearing their footsteps, he turned and faced them, cautiously, as he did so, fixing an arrow in his bow. The moment he saw them, however, he withdrew it, letting the arrow fall to the ground, and hastened with hurried strides towards them. They now saw that he was indeed a white man, with a flowing long beard, which made him appear older than he really was. He looked from one to the other with an inquiring gaze. Gilbert's heart bounded within him.

"Can it be?" exclaimed the stranger, as he stretched out his arms. "Art thou Gilbert Audley?"

"Yes, father, yes," exclaimed Gilbert, as he sprang forward, and the next instant was clasped to the breast of Captain Audley.

"I had heard that thou wert far off, my boy," said Captain Audley, "and little did I expect to see thee, and was even now on my way to obtain the aid of some of our countrymen, who are not a day's voyage from this, to rescue thee from the hands of those who held thee in bondage. And this is the son of my noble friend, Sir Edward Fenton," he continued, stretching out his hand to Gilbert's companion. A few words sufficed to explain how he knew all this. Gilbert then told him of their escape from the Indians, and of the probability of their being pursued.

"Then we must not tarry here longer," said Captain Audley, "though I fear that my weary limbs will not carry me as fast over the ground as your young ones have brought you along. It were better for you to hasten on rather than run the risk of being overtaken by the savages."

"No, no, father! having once found you, we will not desert you," exclaimed Gilbert.

"That we will not, sir," said Fenton, "though overtaken by a whole host of pursuers, we shall be three to oppose them, while we may use a stout tree as a fortress, behind which we may find shelter, and with fire-arms in our hands, while our ammunition lasts we may keep at bay any number who may come against us."

"We will rather strive to avoid them without shedding of blood," said Captain Audley; "I have seen so much slaughter since I have dwelt among these benighted savages that I pray I may live and die in peace, without being compelled to draw another drop of blood from the veins of my fellow-creatures—but on, lads, on, we must not longer waste the time when relentless foes are following us, and sure I am that the savages will not allow you to escape without an attempt to recover you."

Saying this, Captain Audley took his son's arm, and together they hastened on in the direction they had before been proceeding. Still, as he had said, he found that he could not run at the speed at which they had been going. Both Gilbert and Fenton, however, endeavoured to assure him that it was fast enough to enable them still to keep ahead of their pursuers. In this, however, they were wrong: scarcely had they proceeded more than a league when Gilbert, striking his foot against a root, stumbled, and as he recovered himself, turning his head he saw a large band of Indians appearing above the brow of a slight hill they had crossed half a mile or so back. The cry he uttered made his companions look in the same direction.

" We shall have to try your plan, Fenton," he said in a tone which lacked not cheerfulness. " Father, under your eye we shall fight with confidence."

" We have time, at all events, to choose our ground," said Captain Audley, looking round; "yonder tree by the river's bank will serve our purpose, and at the last, should your ammunition fail, and my arrows all be shot away, we may plunge into the stream and swim along it till we gain the opposite bank, whence we can float down the current on a raft till we meet our countrymen, encamped, as I hear, some leagues on—though I know not their exact position." This was said as they were making their way towards a huge tree the roots of which projecting far into the water, left the ground on the near side sufficiently smooth to enable them to slip round it for the purpose of firing. As they had seen the Indians, they knew that they must themselves have been discovered. They had but little time to wait, for the savages with loud cries were rapidly approaching, exhibiting on their spears the scalps they had that morning taken from their unsuspecting foes, surprised in the village.

Gilbert and Fenton quickly loaded and stood

ready to fire directly an arrow should be drawn against them. The savages, however, having got almost within range of their pieces, halted, unwilling to expose themselves to the deadly balls, of whose searching power they had so much dread. Gilbert, who lay sheltered by a high root, observed the larger portion of them moving away to the left, evidently with the intention of surrounding the tree which now afforded them shelter.

" The cunning redskins think they have us in a trap," he said ; " but the tree will still serve our purpose, and those who approach will pay dear for their boldness."

The Indians, however, still kept at a distance, though he caught sight of them moving round the clumps of trees towards the east. He and Fenton stood ready with their pieces to pick off the first who should venture near enough to be reached. At length they appeared, advancing under such shelter as the trees afforded, each Indian with an arrow in his bow ready to shoot.

" Now," cried Gilbert, " my piece covers one of their chief men ; have you marked another ? "

The Indians at that instant set up one of those fearful yells which they use to intimidate their foes. It was replied to by a cheer which could come from none but British throats.

" Stay," cried Captain Audley," we shall be saved without firing a shot : here come our friends."

The Indians heard the cheer, and casting their

eyes down the stream, instantly sprang back to regain the shelter they had just quitted. A few shots were heard fired among the trees, which considerably hastened their flight, though none were hit, and long before the boat pulling against the current could reach the tree, every Indian on that side had disappeared, while the rest were seen retreating at full speed towards the hill over which they had come. Captain Audley and his companions now hastened on to meet the boat. The first person who sprang on shore was Vaughan, who knew him even before Gilbert had time to shout, " Here is our father!"

They were all quickly on board, for though some proposed following the Indians, Captain Audley urged them to spare those who could no longer injure them, and might, he hoped, with proper treatment become their friends. Having greeted Roger and Oliver, and thanked them and their followers for the exertions they had made to rescue him, he proposed that they should forthwith descend the river and get speedily on board the *Rainbow*. He explained that Wamsutah had willingly released him on his promise to send back a ransom. Having stopped for a brief space of time to bid farewell to Oncagua, promising him also a present to console him for the loss of Virginia, they continued their voyage down the river, the rapids, under Ben's pilotage, being passed in safety.

As may be supposed, they received a warm greeting from Captain Layton, who declared that the satisfaction he felt at the recovery of his old friend was the greatest he had ever enjoyed. The *Rainbow* was immediately got under weigh, and without the loss of a single member of her crew, and with the recovered ones on board, in addition to the young maiden, she returned to James Town.

CHAPTER XIII.

ORDS would fail to describe the meeting of Captain Audley with his wife and daughter. Mistress Audley, could tell her husband that she had been buoyed up, not by false hopes, but by trusting One who orders all for the best; and their hearts were lifted up in gratitude to Him Who had seen fit to reunite them on earth; albeit, having the same blessed faith, they had looked forward to a joyous meeting in Heaven. Vaughan soon after returned, and became the husband of Cicely; but Lettice had to undergo another trial. Captain Layton had to fulfil his promise to his crew to go in search of a Spaniard, the object of his previous adventure being accomplished. He was not a man to swerve from his word, although he would fain have remained at the settlement, and enjoyed that rest which those advancing in life desire. It happened one evening that as Roger and Gilbert were walking along the banks of the river, they caught sight of a small boat pulling rapidly down the stream, with two men in her. Directly afterwards they encountered Fenton.

" I have just seen that fellow Flowers shove off with another man," he said, " and when I demanded

where they were going, he would give me no answer.
He has been holding correspondence with a strange
Indian who came up from the mouth of the river,
and has since been trying to gain over several of
the ill-disposed in the settlement, for some object
which has not transpired."

" Then let us follow him," exclaimed Roger, " the
Rainbow's boat is near at hand, and we may speedily
overtake the traitor, if traitor he is."

They hastened on board the *Rainbow*, and wisely
putting some provisions and water into the boat,
pulled away in chase of Flowers. The skiff possessed
by the latter was a fast one, and though they pulled
on all night they failed to come up with her. Sometimes they thought that they must have passed her;
if so, they hoped to meet her as she was coming
down at daylight. Just as they were nearing
Hampton Roads, they caught sight of a stout ship
standing out past Old Comfort Point, with the skiff
of which they were in search towing astern. They
immediately redoubled their efforts ; but before they
could come up with her, the breeze freshening, she
stood away out to sea.

" That craft is a Spaniard, though she shows no
colours," exclaimed Roger.

" No doubt about it, sir," observed Ben Tarbox,
who was pulling the stroke oar, " and that accounts
for why Master Nicholas was praising the Spaniards.
To my mind he is half a Spaniard himself; I thought
no good would come of his beads and his crosses,
his paters and aves."

"What; was he a Romanist, then?" asked Gilbert.

"As arrant a one as I ever set eyes on," replied Ben; "and, if he had had his will, he would have liked to make us all Romanists too, and burn us at the stake, as they did in Mary's time."

"He is welcome to his religion," said Roger, "but if he is playing false to the settlement, he will have yet to repent it. Lads, we must hasten back on board the *Rainbow*, and go in chase of yonder Don. If she has any evil design, she will be hovering round the coast for some time to come."

His proposal was received with a loud cheer, and the crew giving way, the boat, aided by the flood-tide, pulled back to James Town. The *Rainbow* was ready for sea, with the captain on board. A short note to Lettice, telling her that they had gone to catch the Don, and not omitting such expressions of affection as his heart prompted, was all Roger had time to write. The breeze being fair, and the river now well known, the *Rainbow*, under all sail, was soon rounding Old Comfort Point. She had not got far down the Chesapeake when a sail was seen ahead, standing to the southward, which made Captain Layton and his crew only the more eager to come up with her. For all that night and the next day the chase continued; but the *Rainbow* kept the Don in sight, and, ere evening closed in, ranged up on her quarter, firing a broadside and receiving hers in return.

"We'll make short work of it, lads," cried the captain, ordering the helm to be put to starboard, and running on board the Spaniard. Grappling-irons secured her, and, led by Roger, the British crew were quickly on her deck. Among the Spaniards was seen Nicholas Flowers, fighting desperately ; but they could not long withstand British muscle and valour, and, ere five minutes were over, the Spanish ensign was hauled down, her crew cried for quarter, and the patache *Nuestra Señora del Pilar de Saragossa* became a prize to the *Rainbow*.

She was richly laden, with a large store of provisions on board ; these, with the best part of her lading, and all her arms and ammunition, were transferred to the *Rainbow*. The captain having no wish to detain the survivors of her officers and crew, they were allowed to go on board, with sufficient provisions to carry them back to their own country, provided they were not captured by a Salle rover on their homeward voyage. The *Rainbow* having seen *Nuestra Señora del Pilar de Saragossa* safe out of the harbour, with her teeth thus drawn, proceeded up the river, carrying Master Nicholas Flowers and his companion, one Dick Trunnion, who swore that he had been beguiled to undertake the adventure by Nicholas, not knowing his object. He, moreover, declared that Master Nicholas was the very man who had piloted the Armada which came so proudly to conquer England, dethrone the queen, and establish the Holy Inquisition in the land ; and

that he had plotted to deliver up the settlement to
the Spaniards, who would speedily have committed
all the heretics who declined to conform to their
faith to the flames. On their arrival at James Town,
Master Nicholas was delivered over to the authorities, and his guilt being proved, he was hanged
on board a ship in which Sir Thomas Gates shortly
afterwards returned to England. The arms were
claimed by the authorities; the rich lading of the
prize was divided among the crew of the *Rainbow*,
the officers coming in for their share.

"Lads," said Ben Tarbox, as the division of the
spoil was being made, "there is a young maiden
whom we all know in the settlement, the firstborn
here, and the only one alive of our countrymen and
countrywomen who once dwelt in the land. She is
dowerless and friendless, except her young brother
and an old grandfather, who maybe sleeps in his
grave by this time. I am ready to give half of my
share, and I invite those among us who have no kith
or kin to give up such portion of theirs as they may
think fit; being very sure that it would be thus
better expended than it will be after the fashion
many of us are apt to get rid of our rhino. Those
who think with me hold up their hands, and those
who don't, keep theirs in their pockets."

Ben's appeal was liberally replied to, and no one
refused to give a handsome portion of his share to
the fatherless orphan.

Meantime, Mistress Lettice had been labouring
diligently to instruct the uncultivated mind of

Virginia, who rapidly improved under her tuition. From no one, however, did she obtain so much instruction as from her brother, who, during every moment he could spare from his duties, devoted himself to teaching her. Her astonishment at seeing the lovely Pocahontas, dressed in the English fashion, and possessing far more knowledge of English customs than herself, knew no bounds, and instigated her to still greater exertions; so that, ere long, she distanced the young bride in book-learning, if not in other accomplishments. Harry Rolfe, indeed, at length became persuaded that, while his wife remained in the country, she would make but slow progress in such accomplishments as he wished her to acquire, and resolved to take her to England. Mistress Audley warned him of the danger of transplanting the flower of a southern region to a northern clime; but he disregarded her admonitions, and sailed some months after his marriage. News then came of the admiration his young bride, the beautiful savage, as she was called, excited at court; then, that she had given birth to a son, and afterwards, that she and her husband were about to return. But, alas! by the next ship came the account of her early death; though Harry brought back his boy to the land of his adoption, regretting that he had ever left it.

Roger had for some time been rewarded with the hand of Lettice, but the old captain, discontented, as many were, with the state of the colony, proposed to return to his old home on the shore of Plymouth Sound, still kept up by his faithful steward Barnaby Toplight. Captain and Mistress Audley, hearing of his intentions, the former especially longing to see once more his native land, determined to accompany him. Roger and Lettice, though not weary of the colony, were unwilling to let him go alone to a solitary home, and he gladly accepted their offer to return with him. Virginia had daily grown in their affections, and as they felt sure that her presence would cheer the declining days of her grandfather, they invited her and Oliver to accompany them, it being settled that the latter should return after a time to Vaughan, should he so wish.

The *Rainbow* arrived safe in England; Oliver and his sister were affectionately received by their grandfather. From that day forward he would scarcely part from Virginia, so completely did she entwine herself round his heart.

"Ah!" she used to say, "I obeyed my Indian grandfather, Oncagua, from fear; but I like to do what you tell me because I love you, and you are so kind."

She little thought how firmly her image remained impressed on the stern warrior's heart, of which he afterwards gave a strong proof.

Oliver and Virginia remained with the old man, who, however, worn out by age and disappointment, died in their arms, tended dutifully by them to the last. Oliver had long desired to go back to the colony·

his sister refusing to be separated from him, and her education being now considerably advanced, they obtained the sanction of Mistress Audley to return thither. They sailed in the *Rainbow,* under the command of Roger Layton.

While he was away, the old captain invited Mistress Audley and her husband to stay with him and their daughter; a home they never afterwards quitted, as Captain Layton dying, they lived on with Lettice and Roger, who gave over the command of the ship to Fenton; for Gilbert had settled with his brother in the colony. Having established a home, he persuaded Virginia, ere long, to become its mistress.

CHAPTER XIV.

OME years passed away. Powhattan was dead; the Indians appeared as friendly as ever, but the tie which had bound them to the palefaces was broken.

Several towns and villages had sprung up in various directions; some on the banks of the river below James Town; others some way above it, in the interior. Among these was Williamsburg, which had been founded on the spot where Rolfe and his party had been attacked by the Indians, when by Canochet's timely warning they had been so providentially saved from being cut off. The whole face of this part of the country was now completely changed; comfortable dwellings, orchards, gardens, and fields covered the ground before occupied by the dark forest, while a bridge was thrown over the stream, which was usefully employed in turning a mill to grind the corn of the settlers. Among the principal people in the neighbourhood was Vaughan Audley, who resided on an estate about three miles from the town, while Gilbert and his young wife had been for some time established in a cottage close to Williamsburg. Their old friend Fenton never failed to pay them a visit when the *Rainbow* came to James Town to bring them news of their relatives at home, as also the various necessaries they required from the old country. They were, as has been said, on the best of terms with the Indians, who came frequently into the town, mixing freely with the settlers, often bringing presents of deer and wild turkeys which they had shot, and fish which they had caught in their streams, and those fruits which abounded in their forests. Even those who at one time had been looked upon as enemies now took much pains to show the settlers that they wished to live in amity with them. Thus were lulled any suspicions the English might have entertained of the natives, and they fondly hoped that they were to retain peaceful possession of the country. `

Virginia was seated with her husband one evening, when a dark form appeared at the open door. "Manita," said a voice, "one who held you to his bosom when you were still a helpless infant comes to warn you and him whom you love of a sudden and fearful danger. Escape with me, and I will protect you—remain, and your doom is sealed."

"Who are you, that we should thus trust you?" asked Gilbert.

"Oncagua," answered the Indian; "she once knew me; does she forget me now?"

"Oh, no, no!" exclaimed Virginia, starting up and grasping the Indian's hands, which she placed on her head; "my ever kind protector; I should indeed be ungrateful could I have forgotten you. What my husband desires, I will do."

"We thank you, chief," said Gilbert, "but we have friends here whom we cannot desert; whatever may be the danger, we must remain and share it with them."

The chief stood lost in thought. "I understand you," he said, "you are right. I came to save her alone, but her friends must be my friends. Tell them to be prepared for a sudden attack from the surrounding tribes, or ere another sun has set not a paleface in the country will be left alive. I know no one I would entrust my message to, but have journeyed night and day, across streams, and through

R

forests, and over hills to utter the warning. Swear that you will follow my advice, or I will stay and perish with you."

Virginia, knowing that Oncagua spoke the truth, entreated Gilbert to do as he wished. He no longer hesitated; and the old chief, taking another fond look at Virginia, disappeared from the door-way.

Happily, Oliver Dane, who lived with Vaughan Audley, was expected that evening to pay them a visit. Anxiously they waited his arrival. Virginia could not help fearing that the Indians might have attacked him on the way, and Gilbert was equally alarmed for Vaughan and Cicely's safety.

"I cannot leave you, dear one, alone," he said; "and yet there is not a moment to be lost."

"Do not fear for me," she answered. "Go and warn our neighbours,—persuade them to put the town into a state of defence. I will wait here till Oliver arrives, and give him such directions as you may leave with me."

Gilbert sat down with his hands on his brow, considering what steps it would be necessary to take; for the lives of all the inhabitants of the colony might depend upon his decision, should no one else have received a warning of what was about to occur. His plans were quickly formed; he must immediately despatch to James Town and other places further off bold and trusty messengers to induce the inhabitants to take proper measures for their preservation; while he himself determined to collect a body of friends, and to hasten as fast as their steeds could carry them to the assistance of Vaughan, leaving Oliver for the protection of Virginia. It cost him much to decide thus, but he intended to try and persuade Vaughan and Cicely to accompany him back to the town rather than to attempt defending the house, which was ill-calculated to resist a prolonged attack by the Indians. It took him but a brief space of time to arrive at this decision. Hastily buckling on his sword, placing his pistols in his belt, and taking down his gun from the wall, he stood ready to set out.

At that instant Oliver, now grown into a fine young man, arrived. Gilbert briefly told him of the warning brought by Oncagua, and explained the measures he intended to take.

"Oh! let me accompany you to Vaughan's," exclaimed Virginia, when she heard of his intention to go there. "I shall be of assistance to Cicely and her little ones, and I cannot bear the thoughts of being separated from you at a time of such fearful peril."

"If she wishes it, I will place a pillion on my horse, and she can ride behind me," said Oliver. "I would far rather fight for my kind friends than remain behind; and I doubt whether the peril to her will be greater should she accompany us than should she remain behind."

To this Gilbert consented; and while Oliver went to prepare the steeds, he sallied forth to find the principal persons, to whom it was necessary to impart the information he had received. Scarcely had he got ten paces from the house when a voice, which he recognized as that of his old friend Fenton, hailed him.

"You have, indeed, arrived most opportunely," he said, as he grasped Fenton's hand; and then taking him by the arm, hurried him along with him while he detailed what he had heard, and the proceedings he intended to adopt. "We want a man of courage and judgment to take command of the town, and I can answer for it that you will do so. People will obey you," he added.

"In truth, I was on my way to tell you and Vaughan of a warning I myself received this morning, on my arrival in the river, from our old friend Canochet," answered Fenton. "Scarcely had I dropped my anchor than he came on board from the southern side and desired to see me privately in the cabin. He then told me that his tribe were friendly, but he had just cause to doubt the Indians of Powhattan's country, and that although he could not give me any definite information, he was very sure a speedy outbreak was in contemplation. He advised that I should induce my friends to come on board the *Rainbow*, and to sail away immediately. He quickly returned on shore, and I hastened to inform the Governor of what I had heard. Your messenger will, I trust, induce him to take more determined measures for defending the town than he might otherwise have thought necessary."

Captain Fenton's arrival was of great assistance to Gilbert in winning his fellow-townsmen to a sense of their danger. The chief magistrate immediately sent round and summoned all the adult population of the place to meet him without delay. Letters were then despatched to James Town and in other directions with the request that those who received them would send on the warning to places further off. Gilbert then asked for volunteers to accompany him to the assistance of his brother. Four only appeared,—indeed, the magistrate afforded no encouragement for the men to go, wishing to keep them for the defence of the place. Gilbert was in despair, when a grey-headed old man on a rough pony, armed with a big gun, a cutlass, and a huge pair of pistols, came clattering up to the council-house.

" What ! " he exclaimed, when he heard Gilbert's last appeal; " are none of you ready to go and help the daughter and son-in-law of my old commander, Captain Amyas Layton ? And from what I hear, they and their young children will be put to death unless a dozen or more true men are ready to fight in their defence. You all know me, Ben Tarbox,—some of you knew my old captain, and have sailed with him, too,—I don't want to weaken the defence of the town, but I ask for just a few stout hands who will defend Master Audley's house ; and when the Indians find that we can keep them at bay, as I am sure we shall, they'll not think it worth while to come and attack the town."

Ben's appeal was responded to by even more men than he required. He chose eight, which, with the four who had before volunteered, himself, Gilbert, and Oliver, made fifteen, all well armed. As they expected to find four men at least with Audley, they would muster twenty—a number sufficient, inside a log-built house, to withstand a whole host of Indians.

A considerable portion of the night was spent before they were all ready to set out. Gilbert found Virginia and Oliver ready to mount, and without loss of time they commenced their journey. Those on foot were hardy, active men, who could almost keep pace with their horses for the distance they had to go. Gilbert was vexed at the delay which had occurred, lest in the mean time, eager to com-mence their work of slaughter, the Indians might have attacked the house. He and Oliver, riding on either side of Virginia, accompanied by Ben and the rest of the horsemen, pushed on, leaving the men on foot to follow as fast as they could. The horses' hoofs were scarcely heard on the soft ground. They had got almost within sight of the house, when Gilbert caught sight of the figure of an Indian running at full speed. Another and another started up. It was evident they had been taken by sur-prise. Gilbert called to his companions, who dashed on ; but the Indians turning into the still uncleared forest on the right, were lost to sight. Their flight, and the hour they were on the road, showed that their intentions were evil.

"They were probably waiting till the family should come out of the house in the early morning to set upon them," observed Gilbert to Oliver. "Thank Heaven we are in time to prevent their design."

Though anxious to place Virginia in safety, he was doubting whether, with the enemy so close at hand, it was not his duty to wait for the rest of the party on foot.

"No, no, Master Gilbert; you go on and get the young lady safe inside the house, and I'll trot back and let our friends know that there are Indians abroad, so that they may not be taken by surprise," cried Ben, who, not waiting for an answer, set off at once ; while Gilbert and the rest of the horsemen galloped on, closely surrounding Virginia, till they reached the front of Vaughan's house. Gilbert's shouts quickly awakened Vaughan, who, recognizing his brother's voice, hastened down to the door. In a few words Gilbert explained the reason of their coming to his brother, who having had no suspicions of the Indians, confessed that he should have admitted them into the house without hesitation. The appearance of the Indians in the neighbourhood decided him on remaining to defend his house, instead of seeking for protection in the town, as Gilbert had at first proposed. The horses were immediately taken round to the back of the house, and, as they would certainly be killed if left in the stables, they were all brought inside and placed in an unfurnished room.

" I am indeed grateful to you, my brave sister-in-law, for thus coming to my help," exclaimed Cicely, as she embraced Virginia.

Vaughan and Gilbert, with the other gentlemen, and the labourers who had slept in the house, immediately set to work to block up all the lower windows and doors, only leaving sufficient loopholes for their muskets. Every receptacle they possessed for holding water was also filled from the well, both to afford them the means of quenching their thirst and to enable them to extinguish any fire which might burst forth. While they were thus employed, Ben's voice was heard announcing the arrival of himself and the party on foot, who were at once admitted at the back entrance. To prevent the Indians from finding shelter in the outhouses, they were, under Ben's superintendence, quickly pulled down, the materials enabling them still further to fortify the house.

Daylight found them still busily occupied. The fact of their not being as yet attacked convinced them that it was but a small party of Indians they had surprised ; probably they, however, would summon a larger body, should they have determined to attack the house. The garrison were anxious to ascertain if their foes were near; but the stealthy way in which the Indians are accustomed to approach an enemy made it dangerous to send out scouts, who would almost to a certainty have been cut off. Oliver and Gilbert, however, took post by turns on the roof, whence they could obtain a view round on every side, and get sight of the Indians should they draw near.

The morning passed away in perfect quiet; the hour indicated by Oncagua was approaching,—Gilbert only hoped that other places were as well prepared as they were. Dinner had been partaken of, and most of the men, who had been up all night, were lying down to obtain the rest they needed, when Oliver, looking through a trap which opened on the roof, exclaimed, "They are coming!"

The next instant the word was passed through the lower rooms,—the men sprang to their feet, and each one hastened to his appointed post. They had not long to wait, for issuing from the border of the forest appeared a large band of Indians adorned with war-paint and feathers.

"I only wish we had one of the *Rainbow's* guns mounted on the roof, and we'd pretty soon make those fellows put about ship," exclaimed Ben, when he saw them. It was almost impossible to count the Indians as they spread out on either hand, but Gilbert calculated that there were at least several hundreds of them. Trusting to their numbers, they came on fearlessly, uttering their dreadful war-whoops.

"Wait till I give the order to fire," cried Gilbert, who, at Vaughan's request, had taken command. "Let not a shot be thrown away, nor a word be spoken."

The Indians came on, again and again uttering those terrific whoops, but no reply was made. They

might have supposed that the house was untenanted;
still they advanced till they got within range of
the garrison's fire-arms.

" Go back whence you came, or advance at your
peril," shouted Gilbert.

The Indians replied by a shower of arrows.

" Now fire, my lads," cried Gilbert, and all the
men having collected on one side, discharged a
volley which brought well nigh a score of Indians
to the ground. The rest waverd, though they did
not fly. Time was thus afforded to the garrison to
reload, and another volley almost as destructive as
the first was fired. Many sprang back and gazed
around with looks of astonishment, supposing
that the defenders of the house were twice as
numerous as was the case. Still, urged on by their
chiefs, they discharged another flight of arrows, but,
shot at random, they caused no injury. Gilbert
again ordered his men to fire, but the Indians, as
they looked round and saw so many of their tribe
struck down on the ground, were seized with a
panic, and as the bullets again flew among them,
they turned and fled.

Some of the party proposed mounting their
horses and following them up, but Gilbert advised
that they should retain their advantageous post, as
it was probable that the Indians would rally and
return to the attack. They had, however, received
a lesson not easily forgotten, and where they had
expected to overcome a few unprepared people, they
had met with a determined resistance. Great reason

had Gilbert to be thankful to Oncagua for his timely warning. A vigilant watch was kept during the night, but no enemy appeared.

The next morning one of their party volunteered to set off to the town, and in a short time he came back with the intelligence that it had been assailed by the enemy, who had been driven back with great slaughter. James Town in the same way had been preserved; but in a few days sad news came from the remote ones, where, before the messengers arrived the Indians had begun to put into execution the sanguinary plan they had conceived for the destruction of all the palefaces in the country, and several hundreds were massacred. More ships arriving shortly afterwards with fresh settlers, a fearful retribution overtook the Indians, and the country which once they called their own knows them no more.

Gilbert, grateful to the old chief for the service he had rendered, despatched Oliver Dane at the head of an expedition by water to invite him to James Town, where he might be safe from the vengeance of his countrymen, should they discover that he had warned the English of their intended treachery. Oliver returned in two weeks, bringing Oncagua with him. " The old chief has come, at your call," he said, " though my days on earth are few; but ere I go, I would gain more of the wonderful knowledge which changed my Manita into what I now see her; and that, more than the fear of my foes, induced me to accept your invitation."

From that day forward Oncagua seldom went beyond the house and surrounding garden. He gained, however, knowledge he did not seek, for Virginia, aided by Cicely, laboured diligently to instruct him in the truths of the Gospel, and ere he was summoned from earth he could exclaim with confidence " I know that my Redeemer liveth."

The trials and dangers through which our various friends had gone, had taught them also an important lesson, to put their trust in their loving Father, all mighty to save, and gratefully to acknowledge from their own experience that whatsoever He orders is for the best.

THE END.

WYMAN AND SONS, PRINTERS, GREAT QUEEN STREET, LONDON, W.C.

www.ingramcontent.com/pod-product-compliance
Lightning Source LLC
Chambersburg PA
CBHW030132060726
47499CB00015B/1594